Erle Stanley Gardner and The Murder Room

>>> This title is part of The Murder Room, our series dedicated to making available out-of-print or hard-to-find titles by classic crime writers.

Crime fiction has always held up a mirror to society. The Victorians were fascinated by sensational murder and the emerging science of detection; now we are obsessed with the forensic detail of violent death. And no other genre has so captivated and enthralled readers.

Vast troves of classic crime writing have for a long time been unavailable to all but the most dedicated frequenters of second-hand bookshops. The advent of digital publishing means that we are now able to bring you the backlists of a huge range of titles by classic and contemporary crime writers, some of which have been out of print for decades.

From the genteel amateur private eyes of the Golden Age and the femmes fatales of pulp fiction, to the morally ambiguous hard-boiled detectives of mid twentieth-century America and their descendants who walk our twenty-first century streets, The Murder Room has it all. >>>

The Murder Room
Where Criminal Minds Meet

themurderroom.com

T0352399

Erle Stanley Gardner (1889-1970)

Born in Malden, Massachusetts, Erle Stanley Gardner left school in 1909 and attended Valparaiso University School of Law in Indiana for just one month before he was suspended for focusing more on his hobby of boxing that his academic studies. Soon after, he settled in California, where he taught himself the law and passed the state bar exam in 1911. The practise of law never held much interest for him, however, apart from as it pertained to trial strategy, and in his spare time he began to write for the pulp magazines that gave Dashiell Hammett and Raymond Chandler their start. Not long after the publication of his first novel, *The Case of the Velvet Claws*, featuring Perry Mason, he gave up his legal practice to write full time. He had one daughter, Grace, with his first wife, Natalie, from whom he later separated. In 1968 Gardner married his long-term secretary, Agnes Jean Bethell, whom he professed to be the real 'Della Street', Perry Mason's sole (although unacknowledged) love interest. He was one of the most successful authors of all time and at the time of his death, in Temecula, California in 1970, is said to have had 135 million copies of his books in print in America alone.

By Erle Stanley Gardner
(titles below include only those
published in the Murder Room)

Perry Mason series

The Case of the Sulky Girl
(1933)
The Case of the Baited Hook
(1940)
The Case of the Borrowed
Brunette (1946)
The Case of the Lonely
Heiress (1948)
The Case of the Negligent
Nymph (1950)
The Case of the Moth-Eaten
Mink (1952)
The Case of the Glamorous
Ghost (1955)
The Case of the Terrified
Typist (1956)
The Case of the Gilded Lily
(1956)
The Case of the Lucky Loser
(1957)
The Case of the Long-Legged
Models (1958)
The Case of the Deadly Toy
(1959)
The Case of the Singing Skirt
(1959)

The Case of the Duplicate
Daughter (1960)
The Case of the Blonde
Bonanza (1962)

Cool and Lam series

The Bigger They Come (1939)
Turn on the Heat (1940)
Gold Comes in Bricks (1940)
Spill the Jackpot (1941)
Double or Quits (1941)
Owls Don't Blink (1942)
Bats Fly at Dusk (1942)
Cats Prowl at Night (1943)
Crows Can't Count (1946)
Fools Die on Friday (1947)
Bedrooms Have Windows
(1949)
Some Women Won't Wait (1953)
Beware the Curves (1956)
You Can Die Laughing (1957)
Some Slips Don't Show (1957)
The Count of Nine (1958)
Pass the Gravy (1959)
Kept Women Can't Quit (1960)
Bachelors Get Lonely (1961)
Shills Can't Count Chips (1961)

Try Anything Once (1962)
Fish or Cut Bait (1963)
Up For Grabs (1964)
Cut Thin to Win (1965)
Widows Wear Weeds (1966)
Traps Need Fresh Bait (1967)

Cool and Lam series

The D.A. Calls it Murder (1937)
The D.A. Holds a Candle (1938)
The D.A. Draws a Circle (1939)
The D.A. Goes to Trial (1940)
The D.A. Cooks a Goose (1942)
The D.A. Calls a Turn (1944)
The D.A. Takes a Chance (1946)
The D.A. Breaks an Egg (1949)

Terry Clane series

Murder Up My Sleeve (1937)
The Case of the Backward
  Mule (1946)

Gramp Wiggins series

The Case of the Turning Tide
  (1941)
The Case of the Smoking
  Chimney (1943)

Two Clues (two novellas) (1947)

Bachelors Get Lonely

Erle Stanley Gardner

An Orion book

Copyright © The Erle Stanley Gardner Trust 1961

The right of Erle Stanley Gardner to be identified as the author of this work has been asserted in accordance with the Copyright, Designs and Patents Act 1988.

This edition published by
The Orion Publishing Group Ltd
Orion House
5 Upper St Martin's Lane
London WC2H 9EA

An Hachette UK company
A CIP catalogue record for this book is available from the British Library

ISBN 978 1 4719 0912 2

www.orionbooks.co.uk

Chapter 1

I left the elevator, crossed the corridor and opened the door marked COOL & LAM – *Private Investigators.* There was no one in the reception room except the girl at the desk. I nodded to her, walked across to the door marked DONALD LAM – PRIVATE just in time to catch Elsie Brand, my secretary, down on the floor chasing a vagrant newspaper clipping which the wind from the air-conditioning unit had blown off her desk.

The clipping had gone under the desk in a corner, and Elsie was on her hands and knees, reaching for it with one hand.

'Donald!' she exclaimed, and tried to scramble to her feet and keep her skirt over her knees at the same time.

I picked up the newspaper clipping and handed it to her. 'Permit me,' I said.

'Thank you.'

She was reaching for the clipping when the headline caught my eye and I suddenly jerked it back. It had to do with a woman who had been raped and robbed in her apartment. It was the third such incident in three months and there were no clues. The woman had been choked to death with one of her own silk stockings, which had been tied tightly around her neck.

'Any more of these?' I asked.

'I have the clippings of the other two crimes listed under our *modus operandi*. . . . Donald, why do you have me do this?'

'Do what?'

'Keep these scrapbooks dealing with unsolved crimes.'

'It keeps you out of mischief,' I told her. 'Haven't you ever learned that the devil finds mischief for idle hands?'

'Then you'd better do something about *your* hands,' she said. 'And Bertha Cool, your dynamic partner, is impatiently awaiting your arrival.'

'What sort of a humour?'

'Wonderful. I haven't seen her like this in months. She's positively beaming.'

'Someone must have paid a five-dollar fee,' I said. I went on into my inner office, looked over my mail, then walked out past the desk where Elsie was pasting clippings in the scrapbooks.

I paused to look over her shoulder.

She self-consciously raised her hand to her neckline.

'False alarm,' I told her. 'I wasn't even looking. I was looking at the clipping.'

She said: 'You make me nervous when you stand behind me and look down that way.'

'You make me nervous all the time,' I told her. 'What's the idea of saving the clipping about the Peeping Tom in the motel? I told you to save important crimes the police would be really anxious to solve.'

'I know,' she said, 'but I saved this on account of the *modus operandi*. This is the second Peeping Tom case in three days. Both of them were at the same motel, the Swim and Tan Motel at the beach.'

I read the clipping. Agnes Dayton of the Corinthian Arms Apartment at Santa Ana, staying overnight at the motel, had emerged from the shower to encounter a face pressed against the window. She had been too excited to give police other than a vague description, but police had a very good description from another victim, a Helen Corliss Hart, a beauty-shop operator from Phoenix who had had a similar experience with what was presumably the same Peeping Tom three days earlier.

'Routine stuff, but you'd better paste it,' I said to Elsie and went out to the outer office. I jerked my thumb in the direction of my partner's private office and raised my eyebrows. The receptionist shook her head, signifying Bertha had no visitors, so I opened the door and went in.

Bertha Cool was a hundred and sixty-five pounds of steam roller. She was in her late fifties or early sixties, had a glittering eye, a sharp tongue, a gift for profanity and a natural belligerency.

'Donald,' she said, as soon as I had the door closed, 'what the hell's the idea of having Elsie Brand cut all those crime clippings out of the newspapers?'

'It keeps her busy when she has nothing else to do,' I said.

'Well,' she snapped, 'paste and scrapbooks cost money. Why not have her file the clippings in old envelopes? It would be cheaper. . . . And what the hell do you want those clippings for anyway?'

'They're red herrings,' I said.

'What do you mean?'

'When the police crowd us too close on some case, I can dig up a red herring that fits into the general pattern and take off some of the heat.'

'Phooey!' Bertha said. 'You did that a couple of times and now it's become an obsession with you. In the first place, the police aren't going to fall for it that easy, now that they know what you're up to and, in the second place, we aren't going to have any more cases where we get tangled up with the police.'

'What makes you think we aren't?'

'Because I know it. We're going to get this business back on a sound, safe, sane basis of operation. That's the sort of business I was running when you came barging in on my life, with your flair for taking chances on desperate cases, playing tag with the police and turning all the little, routine cases into big-time gambles.

'In those days,' Bertha went on, somewhat wistfully, 'I could sleep nights, I didn't have trouble with blood pressure and ulcers.'

'You also had a note at the bank,' I told her.

'Just the same,' she snapped, '*I'm* going to get this business back to the right kind of a basis! I don't want any more of these tramp clients.'

'What do you mean, "tramp clients"?'

'You know what I mean – these long-legged mysterious women that hover around you like moths around a porch light. Every one of them is a tramp who's got herself involved in something deadly dangerous, and then she comes running to you with a look of mealy-mouthed innocence. . . . Those little bitches know better than to come to me. I can tell what they are a mile off, but you fall for their look of synthetic innocence, their good-looking gams, and their tears.'

'All right,' I told Bertha, 'there's no use arguing this early in the morning. You wanted to see me. What did you want?'

Bertha's face became wreathed in a smile. 'Donald,' she said, 'we've done it.'

'Done what?'

'Started to attract the class of clientele I've always wanted: the big, substantial, solid businessmen who retain us for things that are important but lack the cliff-hanging type of stuff *you* always attract to the office.'

'Tell me about it.'

'His name,' she said, 'is Montrose L. Carson. He is president of the Carson Associates Securities Investment Pool, and the name is deceptive.'

'It should be,' I said. 'With a name like that, a guy could run a bookie joint.'

'Don't be silly. He's the soul of respectability.'

'What does he do?'

'He makes surveys of business properties.'

'Civil engineer?'

'Not that type of survey. He picks out potential business properties, then checks the number of cars that go by each day, the number of persons who walk past the property. He surveys the various adjacent properties, the sort of stores that are in operation, and determines what sort of business would prosper on that corner lot, what is the maximum rental the property should bring.

'When he's done all that, he goes to the owner of the lot and makes a long-term lease, agreeing to put up a building, the title to which will revert to the owner at the end of the lease period.'

'Go on,' I said.

'Well, then he finds someone who is interested in that type of business and makes a proposition to give him the store on a sub-lease. The lease payments are large enough so that the monthly payments on the building come out of the rents and everybody is satisfied.'

5

'Provided the man who runs the business makes a profit,' I told her.

'He does,' she said. 'That's where Mr Carson cashes in. That's the entire secret of his success. The businesses he picks are so carefully chosen that the man who operates the store invariably makes a profit.'

'I take it,' I said, 'that Montrose L. Carson is very efficient. . . . Do you know what the *L.* stands for?'

'Levining. *L-e-v-i-n-i-n-g,*' Bertha said, 'and he *is* exceedingly efficient. Donald, that's the sort of business we should cater to. We should get away from this dangerous business of skirting the walls of the penitentiary.'

'Who's skirting the walls of the penitentiary?'

'Well, you did it in that last case.'

'Phooey,' I said. 'Sergeant Frank Sellers *thought* I was skirting the walls of the penitentiary and sold you on the idea.'

'Well, anyway,' Bertha said, 'this is good, clean-cut business, the sort of stuff we want, working for the big industrial plants. What's more, Mr Carson has some big sub-division stuff going. He has a big one about five miles out of Palm Springs on the road to Indio.'

'All right, what does Montrose L. Carson want?'

'The way he operates,' Bertha said, 'it is necessary that his findings be shrouded in the greatest secrecy.'

'And?' I asked.

'And they aren't.'

'How come?'

'He doesn't know. He wants us to find out.'

'What happens?' I asked.

'One of his rivals,' she said, 'is Herbert Jason Dowling, who operates the Dowling Leasehold Appraisal and Development Company.'

'Go on,' I told her.

'Several times recently when Carson has spent a lot of time and a lot of money making a check on corner lots, fixing the exact potential value of the leasehold, the figures seem to have found their way into Dowling's possession and Dowling has beat Carson to the punch, offering a little more money than Carson was prepared to pay, getting the lease and stealing the whole thing right from under Carson's nose.'

'Probably,' I said, 'Dowling has a system of appraisal that is equally as efficient as that of Carson.'

'The point is, he doesn't,' Bertha said. 'In order to make one of these appraisals it's necessary to get the approval of the police. A small pneumatic hose is put out on the street so that every car going by registers on a counter. Observers watch the number of pedestrians who pass the corner. If two companies were making a simultaneous appraisal, one of the companies would know the other one was there.

'I have covered this situation thoroughly with Mr Carson, and he insists it is a case of their estimates having been communicated to Dowling. He wants us to find the leak in his office.'

'So what?' I asked.

Bertha beamed at me, and her diamonds made coruscating streaks of light as she moved her hands in an expansive gesture. 'It's already taken care of,' she said.

'Go on,' I told her, knowing that Bertha did no leg work and doubting that she would have hired an operative on a job of this sort.

'You are going to be the catalyst,' she said.

'How come?'

'You own a corner lot at Ivy and Deodars Streets.'

'It's a lemon,' I told her, 'a white elephant. I got it on a fee. . . . You didn't want any part of it, so I paid you your share and –'

'I know, I know,' Bertha exclaimed impatiently, 'but the point is Carson is going to juggle his records so that it will appear that that corner lot has been thoroughly examined. His records will show that an exaggerated number of cars pass there each day and a magnified number of pedestrians pass there. The place is going to be marked as a potential filling-station site.

'Now then, there are only four people in the executive office of the Carson company who *could* be peddling information to Dowling. In the strictest confidence, Carson is going to tell these people about your corner lot. He's going to tell one of them that the lot is worth two hundred and fifty dollars a month, one that it's worth three hundred and fifty, one that it's worth four fifty, and one that it's worth five hundred and fifty.

'Now then, if Carson's suspicions are correct, Dowling will send someone to call on you and make you an offer. From the size of the offer, we can tell which one let the figure leak out to Dowling.'

'You mean he's going to come to me here at a detective agency and –?'

'Don't be silly!' Bertha said. 'You won't have anything to do with a detective agency. You'll be a young man who has made enough money to retire on, and this lot is just one of several that you have. You'll be ensconced in a bachelor apartment, apparently living the life of Riley, going to the ball games and the horse races, squiring beautiful women around, and not very much interested in making money. You'll have it made; you've got your pile.'

'The apartment?' I asked.

'Already arranged for,' Bertha said, opening the drawer and taking out a key. 'This is a bachelor apartment in an apartment house owned by Montrose Carson. You'll be in there under your right name, of course, but you won't be too easy to locate.'

'What will I be doing with my time?' I asked.

'Just what you're supposed to be doing as a gentleman of leisure,' Bertha said, 'going to the races and the ball games. . . . Dammit, it makes me mad to think of me slaving here in the office while you're getting your expenses paid going around to ball games, horse races, cocktail lounges and high-class restaurants.'

'Alone?' I asked.

'Most of the time,' Bertha said. 'It will save expenses that way.'

'It looks suspicious,' I told her. 'Dowling wouldn't want to deal with me. I'd better have someone with me.'

'Now, look,' she said, 'don't go running up a big expense account on this thing. Carson has already gone all the way. We're collecting fifty dollars a day for your time, in addition to the fee he's paying the agency for thinking out this scheme.'

'It's a nice scheme,' I said, 'if it works.'

'It'll work,' Bertha said.

'How long do we have to incubate these eggs?'

'They have to hatch within a week,' Bertha said. 'Carson is willing to gamble a week's expense money on the thing.'

'Expenses come high,' I said, 'going to horse races, ball games, taking dames out to –'

'Dammit to hell,' Bertha screamed at me, 'you're not a millionaire! You're just a lousy punk who's got it made and would be interested as hell in an income of two hundred and fifty to five hundred and fifty on that lot. Don't think you're going to play Prince Charming to a bunch of these tramps that –'

'We'd have to pay the women,' I said.

'*What!*' Bertha roared. '*Pay* a woman to be taken out to dinner? What the hell are you talking about?'

'On a business deal,' I said, 'you'd have to pay –'

'Take that calf-eyed secretary of yours,' Bertha said. 'She can't keep her eyes off you. She and her tight sweaters, she and her low-cut blouses! My God— Get the hell out of here. Don't start running up a big expense bill on this. This is big business. This is the kind of stuff we want to cultivate. Go ahead and take Elsie out with you and tell her that she's working; that she orders the cheaper dishes and limits herself to two drinks a night. Keep those expenses *down*!'

'When do I get started?' I asked.

'The sooner the quicker,' Bertha said. 'Carson is letting the word leak out around the office today.'

'How does he know some of his employees who are counting cars and pedestrians don't make the leak?'

'Because they don't have access to the figures. Only four people in his organization have access to the appraised figures and the purpose to which the property is to be used.'

'Well,' I said, 'I'll talk with Elsie and see if she wants to be escorted around under those circumstances.'

'She'll jump at the chance so fast she'll jump right out of that square-necked dress of hers,' Bertha said. 'My God, I should have seen this coming. It'll spoil her for any kind of work, and before she gets done she'll have

her hooks into you and you'll be leading her to the altar
. . . And if she does, the only wedding present you'll
get out of *me* will be a get-well card.

'Now, get the hell out of here and start work!'

Chapter 2

Elsie Brand looked at the menu and said: 'I suppose I *should* have the Salisbury steak at three point two five.'

I said: 'Why not try the filet mignon at five point five oh?'

'Bertha would have a fit.'

'You have to be fed,' I told her.

'Bertha might not think so.'

'You have to keep your resistance up,' I told her.

'Resistance to what?'

'One never knows,' I said. 'It might be disease germs.'

'Are you a disease germ, Donald?'

'No, I'm a virus,' I said. 'I'm more insidious and they don't have any antibiotics.'

The waitress stood over the table and I said: 'Two filet mignons, medium rare. One Manhattan, one dry Martini, the shrimp cocktails, some Thousand Island dressing on the salad.'

She left.

Elsie looked at me and shook her head.

'Don't worry,' I said, 'Bertha will love it. I'll make the expense account read: Dinners – two hamburgers at one dollar and twenty-five cents for both, and I'll put the rest of the bill on for taxi fare.'

'Bertha will want to see the receipt and want to know

why you had to use a taxi when you had the agency car.'

'I'll tell her I was afraid they'd take the licence number on the agency car, that I saw someone snooping around.'

'Donald, do you actually do all those things?'

'What?'

'All those things you say. I can never tell when you're kidding or serious.'

'That,' I said, 'is a good sign.'

'Can you tell me what we're working on at the moment?'

'No. It's highly confidential. All you have to do is be my girl friend.'

'How long am I supposed to have known you?'

'Long enough.'

'Long enough for what?' she asked.

'Long enough to be my girl friend.'

'Platonic, passionate or prospective?'

'Do you always want to look at the road map before you take a trip?' I asked.

'I like to know where the boulevard stop signs are,' she said.

The waitress showed up with the drinks.

'Here's to building up resistance,' I said. 'There aren't any stop signs.'

She started to raise the glass, then lowered it and said: 'Here's to the prospective, whatever it is,' and sipped the drink.

We took a long time over the dinner. I explained to Elsie that Bertha wanted to be sure that when I returned to the apartment-house she was with me.

'Then what?' she asked.

'Then,' I said, 'I ask for mail, then I stall around by the elevator and ask you to come up, and you tell me that you think I'd better take you home.'

'No etchings?'

'No etchings.'

'Why the scene in the lobby?'

'It shows that I am healthy and normal.'

'You mean amorous.'

'I was expressing it delicately,' I told her.

'What would happen if I didn't say you had better take me home and let you persuade me to go up to look at the etchings?'

'There are no etchings and I don't know what *would* happen.'

She toyed with the idea.

'Furthermore,' I told her, 'I'm not taking you home. That's one of the things that Bertha had all planned out. She thinks someone might be watching in the lobby. I'm to play it cool. If you won't come up, I call a taxi-cab and send you home in that.'

'You don't escort me?'

'No.'

'That isn't very courteous or considerate.'

'Bertha doesn't want me to be courteous or considerate, she wants me to be effective.'

'And you're taking orders from her?'

'I'm playing it her way at the start,' I said.

Elsie thought things over while we were driving back to the apartment house.

I entered the lobby, went to the desk, asked if there was any mail, then I put on the act with Elsie by the elevator. Elsie seemed half-way ready to go up to the apartment. There was a mischievous twinkle in her eye and she seemed entirely oblivious of the long-legged blonde that was waiting in the lobby watching us with cool, appraising eyes.

'Oh, come on,' I said to Elsie, 'don't be a prude. I just want to buy you a drink.'

The clerk was elaborately interested in other things, pretending not to listen, but his ears were sticking out a foot.

Elsie hesitated. 'Well . . . I *should* be getting home, Donald . . . but . . .'

I said in a whisper: 'Notice the blonde.'

Elsie lowered her voice. 'I've already noticed her. That's why I think I'd better come up.'

I sighed, raised my voice and said: 'Well, if you insist. I'll get a cab.'

'You aren't going home with me?'

'No. I'll send you home in a cab. I've got fish to fry.

Elsie again seemed on the point of changing her mind. I took her arm, moved her over to the door, put her in a taxicab, gave the cab-driver the address and the money, kissed Elsie good night and walked back to the lobby.

The blonde was waiting for me.

'Mr Lam.'

I looked at her and bowed.

'So she wouldn't go up for a drink?'

I studied the provocative eyes, the corners of the mouth that turned up in just the right sort of a smile.

'No,' I said.

'Well, *I* will,' she told me. 'I have something to discuss that can be said up there better than down here. Do you have Scotch?'

I nodded.

'And soda?'

Again I nodded.

She walked over towards the elevator with me.

The clerk gave one swiftly curious glance, then went about his business again.

After we had left the elevator and I had inserted the key in the door, she said: 'He has big ears.'

'Who?'

'The clerk.'

'He's curious.'

'I'll say he's curious. When I asked for you, he looked me over from head to toe.'

I said: 'He'd have done that anyway.'

She laughed and went over and seated herself on one side of the davenport.

I went out to the kitchenette and mixed a Scotch and soda, poured myself some gin and tonic and came back with the drinks.

She crossed her long legs and showed lots of stocking. 'I suppose,' she said, 'you're wondering about me?'

'And, I suppose,' I told her, 'you're wondering about me.'

'I guess that's the way people get acquainted, isn't it, sort of sparring for position?'

'Just what position,' I asked, 'are you sparring for?'

She laughed at that and said: 'I might ask *you* that question.'

'I asked you first.'

'All right. I have a business proposition.'

'Such as what?'

'You own a corner lot on Ivy and Deodars Streets.'

'You have ideas about it?'

'I have ideas about it. . . . Do you have ideas?'

'About the lot?' I asked.

'About the lot,' she said.

'I have *lots* of ideas,' I told her.

'I'm talking about the lot.'

'I'm talking about *lots* – of ideas.'

'How would you like to lease it?'

'Well, I don't know,' I told her. 'I have been thinking some of building and –'

'That would cost you money.'

'Are you in the real estate business?'

'In a way. I'm a sharp-shooter. I bring people together.'

'What sort of a person are you going to bring me together with?'

'Right now it's with me.'

'That suits me,' I told her.

She said: 'Four hundred and sixty-five dollars a month on a long-term lease with a building on the lot that will revert to you when the lease expires.'

'Four hundred and sixty-five,' I said. 'That's a coincidence. I was offered . . . well, I had another offer just a short time ago.'

'I know,' she said. 'Four hundred and fifty. We're beating it fifteen dollars a month. Fifteen dollars a month is a hundred and eighty dollars a year. A hundred and eighty dollars a year would buy lots of things.'

'Such as what?' I asked.

'Flowers,' she said. 'Flowers for the young woman who went home in the taxicab. It might even pay the cab fare – if she insisted on going home every night.'

'And if she didn't?'

'Then a hundred and eighty would come in handy anyway.'

17

'I'll think it over,' I told her.

'How long?'

'Until I make up my mind.'

'My people have some other lots they're figuring on and they'd want to know.'

'How soon?'

'Tomorrow.'

'Isn't this all rather sudden?' I asked.

'Of course it's sudden,' she said. 'That's why I'm here. You're figuring on a deal to put a petrol station on that corner. My people want to get the corner. Not that they care so much about the corner as they do about keeping enough outlets for their petrol so that they can hold their own in a highly competitive market.'

'So they employed you to wait for me here tonight?'

'They employed me to get in touch with you,' she said. 'I inquire at the desk and find that you're out. I arrange with the clerk to point you out when you come in. There's a young woman with you so I certainly don't intrude. If you had made a sale, I'd have waited until tomorrow morning – and if that sounds as though I'm being brutally frank and sophisticated, that's exactly the way I want to sound.'

She shifted her position, crossed her knees the other way, smiled and said: 'And don't get any false ideas, Donald. I'm neither a virgin nor a tramp. I'm a business-woman and I'm here to talk business.'

'I don't know your name yet,' I said.

'Bernice Clinton,' she said. 'In business for myself, free-lancing, unattached and I intend to keep myself that way.

'Now then, you have a corner. There's a deal on for you to lease it and the offer is open until twelve o'clock noon tomorrow, and probably you could get another forty-eight hours for trading, but they have given you until noon on this offer. Right?'

'How do you know all this?'

'Because I'm in a competitive business and we try to know what our competitors are doing. I don't know anything at all about the financing of the thing or the company that is going to make the lease, but I do know that the ultimate beneficiary is a petrol company that is competitive to the company my people represent. We don't want that company to get in your place because we don't want them selling a gallon more petrol than we can help.

'Now then, I've been frank and put my cards on the table.'

'And you're offering?'

'Four hundred and sixty-five.'

'Could you go to four seventy-five?'

She shook her head, watching my expression, then added hastily: 'I don't think so. I could find out and let you know, but I don't think so. I'm prepared to close on four sixty-five right now.'

'We'd have to have lawyers draw up leases and things.'

'Sure,' she said, 'but you could draw up a little note that would be binding and we'd get the formalities cleaned up tomorrow morning.'

'It seems to me it would take a lot of petrol to enable a person to pay that rent, put up buildings and –'

'Leave that to us to worry about.'

She finished the drink and stood up, smoothed her skirt down over the hips and looked at me with a provocative smile. 'Shall we,' she asked, 'go for a nightcap, then come back and seal the bargain?'

I said: 'I'm toying with that idea I put up to you.'

'What idea?' she asked, her eyes instantly wary.

'Four seventy-five.'

'Oh, *that*!'

'That,' I said.

'If you'll make me a definite offer to let me have it at four seventy-five, I'll see what I can do.'

'I don't think I could make a definite offer. I want the offer to come from you.'

'We wouldn't like to make an offer and then have you go to the other people and play one against the other. We don't do business that way. I'm making you a proposition right now.'

'On a take-it-or-leave-it basis?'

'I wouldn't be that crude about it.'

'Well,' I said, 'at the moment, I won't take it. Can I get in touch with you tomorrow morning, say at about ten o'clock?'

She smiled and shook her head. 'Let's say that I'll get in touch with you, Donald. . . . What time do you get up?'

'Around seven-thirty.'

'And what are you going to be doing between seven-thirty and eight?'

'Shaving, eating breakfast.'

'And telephoning?'

'Perhaps.'

'I wouldn't like that,' she said. 'That is, my people wouldn't. So suppose we say my top offer is four sixty-five.'

'And you'll call at ten to get an answer?'

'I'll tell you what I'll do. I'll call on the phone sometime between noon and tomorrow night. You can let me know then what the score is, and now, good night.'

She walked easily and smoothly towards the door. I held it open for her and walked out to the corridor.

' 'Bye now,' she said.

' 'Bye,' I told her.

Chapter 3

Elsie looked up as I entered the office in the morning.

'Was the blonde waiting?' she asked.

'The blonde was waiting.'

'Etchings?'

'I told you I didn't have any.'

'You didn't let me come up to see for myself.'

'You said you weren't coming.'

'You crowded the words in my mouth.'

'I was thinking about the blonde,' I said.

'That,' she retorted, 'was obvious.'

'How's the crime situation this morning?' I asked, changing the subject.

'I'm working on that case where the woman identified the wrong man in the torture rape case,' she said. 'It's horrible.'

'What? The case?'

'No. The identification,' Elsie said. 'The victim positively identified this man. He'd have been convicted if the police just hadn't happened to catch the right individual while they were investigating another crime. The man confessed. Here are the two photographs, side by side. Look at them. There isn't the slightest, most remote resemblance in the world.'

'I know it,' I told her. 'Someday people are going to

wake up to the fact that circumstantial evidence is about the best evidence we have and eye-witness identification evidence is about the worst – particularly when it's handled the way this was.'

'What was wrong with the way it was handled?'

'The girl who had been the victim was lying in a hospital bed, and police first took a photograph and showed it to her. They then asked her if that wasn't the man. She said she *thought* it was. They told her he'd tried an alibi that hadn't stood up and they were pretty positive he was the right man. She thought so, too. A few hours later they brought the man himself into the room. The woman screamed, covered her eyes, and sobbed: "That's the man. That's the man." '

'Well, how else could they have done it?' Elsie asked.

'By using a line-up,' I said. 'An identification isn't worth a darn unless it's made in a line-up, and even then you have to be certain they don't cheat on the line-up. Sometimes they do.'

'Who cheats?'

'The police.'

'Why?'

'Because,' I said, 'the police have a responsibility that goes beyond just catching the individual who perpetrated a particular crime. The police are fighting to keep crimes from happening. They believe a man is guilty and too many times they close their minds. Once they get the idea that a certain person has committed a crime, it's pretty easy for their confidence to engender equal confidence in the mind of the victim. . . . What else is new?'

'Just a lot of routine stuff,' she said. 'You don't want me to save the –'

'Save everything that relates to any series of crimes,' I said. 'I don't care too much about isolated crimes but I do want series crimes, ones where the police haven't been able to catch the perpetrator.'

'And then when they do catch him?'

'Then go back to that book,' I said, 'and make a marginal note that the man was apprehended, tried, and, if he was convicted, make a note of that fact.'

'You're getting the office all littered up with scrapbooks,' she said.

'I think we may be able to use them,' I told her. 'When the police get an idea through their heads they become very single-minded.'

'You mean in relation to one of our clients?'

'Could be.'

'How do you get the idea out of the police mind?'

'You don't,' I said. 'That's the point. You can't. The only thing you can do is to switch your vehicle over to another single track in the police mind and look for a head-on collision.'

She said: 'Donald, you have the most . . . the most impossible ideas . . . the most impudent technique –'

'Stop it,' I told her. 'You're sounding like Bertha Cool now.'

'Fry me for an oyster,' Elsie said, mimicking Bertha Cool's tone.

I grinned at her and went on into my private office.

Ten minutes later I was in Bertha Cool's office with my report.

'The offer,' I said, 'was four sixty-five.'

Bertha's eyes glittered. 'That does it,' she said. 'That pin-points the leak.'

'Who?'

24

Bertha looked at a card that had some names and figures scribbled on it. 'Irene Addis,' she said. 'And she's a relatively new addition to the firm, acts as receptionist and general personal secretary to Carson and to his junior partner, Duncan E. Arlington.'

'So what do we do now?' I asked.

'I ring up Mr Carson and tell him where the leak is in his business.'

'And collect how many days' compensation?' I asked.

'Two.'

I said: 'Somehow that seems awfully easy, Bertha.'

'What's easy?'

'Solving a case like that, that simply.'

'You can solve them all simply if you use your brains.'

'Who else knew about this deal?'

'No one. There were four people who were suspect. I had Carson give each one of them a separate figure. He worked out four false reports with the numbers of automobiles passing the place, an appraisal of the value, the taxes, the zoning and all the rest of it.'

'I don't like it,' I said.

'Why not?'

'It's too easy.'

'You said that before.'

'And you're going to lower the boom on Irene Addis?'

'I'm going to report to our client.'

'And,' I said, 'that's going to be the same as consigning her to the economic scrap heap. She'll be discharged for having betrayed confidential information and she'll never be able to get another job. Anyone who wants a reference from Carson will –'

'Quit being so damn sympathetic,' Bertha said. 'She's got it coming to her.'

'All right,' I told her. 'What about the apartment?'

'Keep it for a month,' Bertha said. 'Use it if you want to for your philandering, but don't let it interfere with your job. That was part of the arrangement. Carson owns the building, but he controls it through a corporation that's a dummy. Your rent was marked paid in advance for thirty days.'

'And, what about keeping up the appearance of being a retired man-about-town?' I asked.

Bertha's face mottled. 'If you're talking about whether or not you can take that moon-eyed secretary of yours out on an expense account every night, I'll give you the answer to that in damn short order. There's no more expense account as of now!'

'Well, it was nice while it lasted,' I said. 'Some agencies would have made it last longer.'

'How much longer?' Bertha asked.

'Until they were sure of what they were doing,' I said.

'Well, I'm sure!' Bertha snapped. 'You get in there and make out that expense account up to date so I can present it to Mr Carson and let's see just how much of a bill you ran up last night – you and your ideas of expenses.'

'I warned Elsie about the champagne,' I said self-righteously.

'About the . . . about the . . . the champagne!' Bertha spluttered.

I walked out and closed the door.

Chapter 4

Elsie Brand, holding a pair of scissors in her hand, a mutilated newspaper in the other, looked up as I re-entered the office and said: 'How's Bertha, and are we still on that case?'

'You buy your own dinner tonight,' I told her, 'and Bertha's mad.'

She made a little face. 'You could have been a little more subtle.'

'Bertha,' I told her, 'doesn't make for subtlety. What's new on the Peeping Tom?'

'Nothing. Have a heart. You can't expect the guy to work every night.'

'I would,' I said.

'Well, perhaps I should have guessed – the way you act about my neckline.'

'A neckline is only a neckline,' I said. 'A woman leaving a shower is a nude. . . . Look back at that first description. See if I could pass muster. I might carry on tonight just to give the police something to work on.'

'Oh, *you*!' she said. 'I wouldn't put it past you at that.'

She turned the pages in the scrapbook. 'Here's the description given by Helen Corliss Hart, the first victim.'

'She's the beauty-shop operator from Phoenix?'

'Right.'

'What's the description?'

Elsie read from the newspaper clipping. 'An older man, about forty-eight, apparently well dressed, with prominent features and bushy eyebrows. I'm afraid you'll have to make a better try than that, Donald.'

I grinned and said: 'Perhaps she took two baths in one evening. Did anyone try to follow you last night?'

'Not a soul. I kept an eye out through the back of the cab window. Donald, I guess I'm never going to make a good operative. I always get a little tingling at the back of my neck when I'm working on a case with you.'

'No tingles otherwise?' I asked.

'Stop it,' she said, smiling. 'Go in there and start answering some of that mail I've piled up on your desk.'

'One should never answer mail,' I told her. 'It means that the people who get the letters you write in answer to the letters they have written answer the letters you have written, and that leads to a vicious circle which causes Bertha to have fits when she sees the amount of the postage bill.'

I went back to my desk, picked up the pile of mail and started reading. There was nothing of any great importance but a couple of routine matters that should be cleaned up so I told Elsie to bring her shorthand book and we'd go to work.

I was midway through the second letter when the door opened and Bertha Cool stood on the threshold, surveying Elsie's crossed knees with hard-eyed disapproval.

I raised an inquisitive eyebrow.

'Montrose Carson,' she said. 'He's in the office and he wants to talk with you. I've been trying to tell him he doesn't need us any more but he thinks he does.'

I winked at Elsie and said: 'Perhaps I can work it so we stay on an expense account tonight, Elsie, and you can get dinner, but this time don't order imported vintage champagne. Just get some of the good domestic –'

'Imported vintage champagne!' Bertha screamed. 'What the hell were you doing last night?'

'Baiting a trap,' I said.

'My God,' Bertha said, 'I could have hired a female operative and saved money. Just because you and your secretary are getting so palsy-walsy, that –'

Elsie interrupted and said: 'He's joking, Mrs Cool. I didn't have champagne at all.'

Bertha glowered at me and said: 'You and your sense of humour. Some day somebody's going to slap you in the kisser.'

'They have already,' I said.

'Well, it hasn't taught you anything. Come in here and meet this guy and, for the love of Mike, remember that this is the sort of business I want to cater to. Your goddam mix-ups with crime are giving me ulcers.'

'What crime?' I asked.

'Just about any case you get mixed into,' Bertha said. 'You attract crime like a magnet attracts iron filings. You're a brainy little bastard, and that's all that keeps you out of the penitentiary. Some day you're going to slip and you'll find you're nothing but a number. Then you won't be spending so much time looking at nylon hosiery.'

Bertha gave Elsie a meaning glance, and Elsie uncrossed her legs and put her knees together.

Bertha turned and strode out of the office.

'I don't think Bertha likes me,' Elsie said.

B

29

'The partnership,' I told her, 'holds you in the highest regard.'

'Any old time,' Elsie said, looking at the door through which Bertha Cool had vanished.

'However,' I went on, 'it's an average. Bertha regards you with less than cordiality, while I make up for it by regarding you with an unsurpassed ardour that –'

Elsie made as if to throw the notebook at me, and I followed Bertha through the door and across the reception room into her private office.

Montrose Carson was somewhere in his forties, slightly stooped, with a long nose, a prominent jaw, and about the keenest pair of eyes I had ever seen on a man. He had a trick of lowering his head slightly so that his eyes, peering out from under heavy grey eyebrows, were intensified. The pupils seemed to be pin-pointed regardless of the light. I could imagine that many a subordinate had quailed under that stare.

Bertha said: 'This is my partner, Donald Lam, Mr Carson.'

Carson gave me a cold, bony hand which felt as though it had been taken out of the ice box, but the grip was strong and firm. His eyes bored into mine.

'Mr Lam,' he said, 'a pleasure.'

'Glad to know you, Mr Carson,' I told him, and sat down.

Bertha said: 'I've told Mr Carson what happened, but he somehow isn't satisfied.'

'I just can't believe that Irene Addis would double-cross,' he said.

'Why, if it's a fair question?' I asked.

'Because she seems like such a nice girl. She is quiet, efficient and yet withal there's a certain vitality about her, a – In short, she's a perfect lady, and yet . . . well, she seems to be intensely human.'

'How old?' I asked.

'I didn't look at her application blank before I came up.'

'Well, you've seen her. You know approximately.'

'Oh, somewhere . . . well, perhaps around twenty-six or twenty-seven.'

'Bertha has explained to you how she determined the lead came from Irene Addis?'

'Yes. She explained it to me earlier. That was all part of the trap. There were four people who might have been passing on the information, and Irene Addis was one of them. I gave each one of those persons a different figure which represented the monthly rental I was willing to pay.'

'How did you handle it in the files?' I asked. 'Couldn't your filing clerk have checked and found there were different figures?'

'I took care of that,' Carson said. 'Duncan Arlington, my partner and vice-president in charge of operations, took the file and kept it locked up in his desk. If anyone had wanted to consult the file to get the traffic survey figures, they would have found a tab showing that it had been removed from the filing cabinet and was being held for Arlington's personal consideration.'

'Then Arlington must have known about it,' I said.

'Certainly he knew about it,' Carson said. 'I wouldn't take a step of this nature without consulting him. In fact, he and I had gone over the situation thoroughly when it appeared there must be a leak out of our office.'

'Why doesn't Herbert Dowling go peddle his own

papers?' I asked. 'Why does he have to keep crowding in on your territory?'

'It's a long story,' Carson said. 'Dowling is the head of a corporation, but he doesn't own the control. At one time it was a partnership. Two of his partners died, but the business was incorporated before their deaths. Now Dowling has something like a third interest, the job of running the corporation, and is faced with the possibility that he may be removed. He's trying to cut operating costs to the bone, yet make a good showing. A stockholders' meeting is coming up, and Dowling wants a five-years contract.'

'You seem to know a lot about him,' I said.

Carson fastened those cold eyes on me from under the heavy eyebrows and said: 'I have made it my business to find out a lot about him.'

'Okay,' I said. 'What do you want us to do now?'

'First, I want you to make absolutely certain,' he said.

'Certain of what?'

'Certain of the information you were retained to get, the source of the leak, the manner in which Dowling is getting the confidential information.

'Now I am willing to admit that there is a prima facie case against Irene Addis. You can, for the moment, forget investigating any of the others, but concentrate on her. Find out her background, her history. Put shadows on her if necessary. See if she has any meetings with Dowling or any representatives of Dowling – but I don't want her to know that she is being shadowed or is under suspicion in any way.

'Do I make myself clear, Mr Lam?'

I nodded.

'Now then, we come to the other question. Who

was the young woman who made the offer to you on Dowling's behalf?'

'Her name was Bernice Clinton,' I said. 'She didn't say in so many words that she was representing Dowling.'

'Quite naturally, she couldn't. The name means nothing to me. Can you describe her?'

'Bernice Clinton,' I said, 'has blue, laughing eyes and blonde hair. I would say she is somewhere around twenty-eight. She has long legs and she has the graceful walk of a long-legged person. She –'

'My interest is not biological,' Carson said, 'it is for the purpose of trying to identify her.'

'A little taller than the average,' I said, 'but not much. A good figure, rather full lips.'

Carson frowned in thoughtful concentration. He was silent for seven or eight seconds, then he slowly shook his head.

'I have made a mental review of the people I know who might have an actual or potential association with Herbert Dowling, and this young woman doesn't ring a bell; that is, her description doesn't.'

I said: 'Remember, you're the one that thinks the offer came from Dowling. I didn't say it did. I simply gave you the circumstances. Bernice Clinton talked about clients whom she was representing.'

'It has to be Dowling,' Carson said.

'All right, that's your conclusion, not ours. You take the responsibility of that decision, we don't – at least until we know more about Bernice Clinton.'

'All right. Find out more about her,' Carson said. 'String her along.'

'All this is costing you money,' I told him.

'Certainly,' he said testily. 'Mrs Cool has been all over that. You don't realize how important this matter is to me. If there is a leak in my organization, I want to find it out.'

'Suppose,' I said, 'it isn't Irene Addis? Suppose it has been made to appear that way?'

'I don't see how it could be. There's no other explanation . . . but –'

'If you're convinced it's Irene Addis, there's no need for us to go ahead with any further investigation,' I said.

He gave a wry smile and said: 'I guess you have me there, Mr Lam. . . . Very well, go ahead. Continue your investigations. "*Leave no stone unturned.*" That is, I believe, the general cliché which applies to a situation of this sort. I want the answer. I want all of the information – no matter who's mixed up in it, I want the answer.'

He shook hands with me, then bowed low over Bertha's hand and said: 'You are a very competent individual, Mrs Cool.'

Then he was gone.

Bertha beamed at the closing door. Then she turned to me. 'Why drag Duncan Arlington into it?' she asked.

'I didn't.'

'The hell you didn't. You kept intimating that someone might be framing this Addis woman and emphasized the fact that Arlington had all the information.'

'All right,' I said, 'what's sacred about Arlington?'

'Nothing,' she said, 'except Irene Addis is the girl we want. She's a double-crossing, scheming little bitch who has been planted in Carson's office as a spy.'

'You're making all of those accusations,' I said, 'simply because you thought up the scheme of the phony figures

34

and Bernice Clinton showed up with the figure nearest the one you assigned for Irene Addis.'

'And that's enough,' Bertha said. 'It's enough to convince anyone. If *you'd* thought of the scheme, you'd have considered it iron-clad.'

'It's not the sort of a scheme I would have thought up,' I said.

'You're damn right, it isn't,' Bertha said. 'You would have insisted on having personal contact with the various individuals. You would have studied Irene Addis, and if she'd been half smart she'd have showed you her legs the way Elsie Brand does, and you'd sit there with that fatuous smile of adulation on your countenance, taking in everything she gave you.'

'It's a shame not to look when the looking is there,' I said.

'You get the hell out of here and find out about Irene Addis,' Bertha said. 'Those are our instructions now. Let's run her down and find out all we can about her.'

'And in the meantime I keep the apartment and keep up the playboy atmosphere?'

'There is no specific authorization for expenses in connection with the matter, but the rent is, of course, paid on the apartment for a month.'

'However, Montrose Carson told me to develop Bernice Clinton.'

'Well, be certain you don't get her over-developed,' Bertha snapped.

I went back to my office and grinned at Elsie. 'I have an idea you're out of the running tonight,' I said. 'I have been instructed to investigate that long-legged blonde who was in the lobby last night and find out what makes her tick.'

'While you're listening to the tick,' Elsie said, 'be careful the alarm doesn't go off.'

'If it does,' I told her, 'I'll press the shut-off button.'

'So as to keep from waking up?' she asked.

'No, so as not to disturb the neighbours.'

'She'll be all run down by that time,' Elsie said acidly.

'So will I,' I said.

Chapter 5

Plain, ordinary leg work is the most prosaic, time-consuming job a private detective can get into.

I put in three-fourths of the day doing leg work.

I called Carson, got him to go into the employment records in the personnel department and dig out the references Irene Addis had given when she started work.

There were four companies she had worked for. I got the names of each and checked up on her. They all gave excellent reports on her character, but there was one period of hiatus. Three years ago she had apparently been out of work for eighteen months. There was nothing to show where she had been during that time.

I got her social security number and started checking back from that. There was information I was not supposed to be able to get, but it was information that could be dug up if a person went at it the right way.

At three-thirty in the afternoon I had the information I wanted. During that eighteen-month hiatus she had been working for Herbert Jason Dowling.

That left me with a puzzle. Why had she failed to list her employment with Dowling when she applied for her next job? Why had she consistently failed to report that employment? Was it because she had been fired for dishonesty?

Apparently none of the personnel departments had seen fit to check into that hiatus in her work record.

At four o'clock I was back in the office.

Elsie Brand said: 'Here's a telegram for you.'

I opened it and read: 'D PURCHASES MYSTERIOUS MONTHLY CASHIERS CHECKS IN AMOUNT ONE HUNDRED AND FIFTY DOLLARS LAST PART OF EACH MONTH. WHY NOT FIND OUT WHAT HAPPENS TO THOSE CHECKS BEFORE MAKING FINAL REPORT TO C. DON'T BE A SUCKER.' The message was signed: 'A FRIEND OF A FRIEND.'

I read the telegram a couple of times, then pushed it down in my pocket.

'A date tonight?' Elsie asked.

'No date. You buy your own dinner.'

I checked out of the office, went to the main office of the telegraph company and found that the telegram had been sent from a branch office in Hollywood.

I filed the telegram under the head of unfinished business, went out to dinner and then put in an evening watching television in my new apartment.

It was nine-thirty when the phone rang. The clerk said: 'Miss Clinton wishes me to ask if you can give her a few minutes on a business matter.'

'Ask her if she'd like to come up,' I said.

A moment later the clerk said: 'She's on her way up, Mr Lam.'

I went out to the elevator to meet her.

'What happened to the cute little girl you were out with last night?' she asked by way of greeting.

'Nothing,' I said.

She laughed at that. 'I didn't mean it that way.'

'You asked it that way.'

'What I meant was I thought you'd be all tied up to-night. I hardly expected to find you here.'

'Then why didn't you telephone?'

'Oh, it's just as easy for me to walk over.'

'Meaning you live in the neighbourhood?'

'Meaning that I need the exercise. I'm watching my figure.'

'It's a habit that's growing on me,' I told her.

'What is, exercise?'

'No, watching your figure.'

She laughed. 'All right. Let's quit the wisecracks, Donald. Invite me in and give me a Scotch-on-the-rocks, not *too* strong.'

'What would be too strong?'

'I don't want to say things I shouldn't.'

'Do you want to do things you shouldn't?' I asked.

'Don't we all?' she asked, and laughed.

'I know I do,' I told her.

'I guess people are all the same under the skin. What about your lot, Donald?'

'What about it?'

'You haven't closed with the other people?'

'No.'

'Are you going to lease it to me?'

'I don't think so.'

'Okay,' she said, 'I guess I'll have to use persuasion.'

'Such as what?'

'Ply you with liquor and let you take me dancing.'

'Do you like to dance?'

'With prospective purchasers.'

'Why not try coming up on the price?'

'Why not try coming down on your demands? That lot isn't doing you any good just sitting there.'

I looked her over and said: 'Just because something is sitting there doesn't mean I don't have plans for it.'

She laughed and said: 'Go get me the Scotch – you certainly are fast on your feet. How about dancing?'

'I want to concentrate.'

'Dancing may help you concentrate.'

'And, again, it might take my mind off of values,' I said.

'Well, what did you suppose I wanted you to dance with me for?'

She got up from the davenport, walked over to a bookcase, fumbled around for a moment, then disclosed a knob that turned on a hi-fi.

'I thought so,' she said. 'That bookcase looked just too damn erudite to be part of an apartment that matched *your* personality.'

She shuffled through the platters, selected one, put it on, kicked a rug to one side with a dainty toe, pirouetted in the middle of the floor and held out her arms as the music started.

I danced with her, and she was like a spider web blowing across the landscape on a hot afternoon.

When the waltz was over she said: 'You do that wonderfully well, Donald. I thought perhaps you'd prefer one of the faster steps – I like waltzing.'

'And Scotch-on-the-rocks,' I said. 'I'll get it for you.'

'I'm not in such a big hurry for that as I was. There's another waltz on that record.'

She hummed for a moment until the needle caught and then we were waltzing again.

She moved over, turned the record off and kissed me. It was a soul-searching, passionate kiss.

'Now,' she said, releasing me, 'I am ready for the Scotch-on-the-rocks.'

I poured a couple of drinks. We sat there drinking them. She had her knees crossed and her toe continued keeping time to the music she'd shut off.

'Do you like me, Donald?'

'Uh-huh.'

'Why don't you loosen up and give my people a lease on that lot . . . now that I've given you the full treatment.'

'I thought there might be more coming if I held out,' I said.

She let her lips harden. 'Well, you made a mistake on that,' she said. 'You've had it all.'

'I didn't mean the full treatment,' I said. 'I meant the rent.'

'Oh,' she said, 'that's different.'

'How much different?'

'How much more do you want?'

I said: 'Other people are in the market for that lot. I want the top price.'

She frowned and said: 'Those other people haven't as yet –' She stopped quickly, as though wanting to bite off the words she'd just said and recall them.

'How do you know they haven't?'

'Have they?'

'I've had a nibble.'

'I'm giving you a bite.'

'Well,' I told her, 'there are as good fish in the seas as have ever been caught.'

'I know,' she said, 'but think about the bird in the hand and the two in the bush.'

'You're the bird in the hand?' I asked.

She looked up in my eyes impudently, audaciously. 'What do you think?' she asked.

'I think,' I told her, 'that I'm beginning to get unduly influenced by your proximity. I'm afraid that I'm slipping. I think that I'm about to fall.'

'That's better,' she said. 'I didn't like to think that I had reached a point where men had become immune to my influence.'

'I put up a valiant fight,' I told her.

'Darned if you didn't – is the answer yes?'

I said: 'It's the proximity that makes this thing delightful. If I said yes, you'd probably be gone within five minutes and I wouldn't ever see you again.'

'My, you have a philosophy of futility.'

'If, on the other hand, I keep this attitude, you're apt to keep up the approach.'

'Until my principal advises me another corner lot has been found that is equally suitable, and then you will never see me again.'

'Never, never, never?'

'Never, never, never,' she said, smiling.

'I have to make a phone call,' I told her.

'What's stopping you?'

'You are.'

'Why?'

'I don't want you to listen.'

'All right,' she said, 'I'll go powder my nose.'

'I'll try the phone booth at the end of the hall,' I said. 'You just make yourself at home and pour more Scotch.'

'I'll go through your personal things, Donald.'

'Do that,' I said.

I went to the hall and took the elevator down to the lobby. There was a taxi at the stand at the corner. I walked over to the driver and handed him twenty dollars.

'What's this for?' he asked.

'Put your flag on waiting time,' I said. 'Pull it up in front of the apartment house. Stand at the desk. Some time within the next five or ten minutes I'll flash a message down to you that a long-legged blonde is on her way out. I want to find out where she goes.'

'No rough stuff,' the cabbie said.

'No rough stuff at all.'

'If she finds out she's being tagged, then what do I do?'

'Turn around and come back. Otherwise she'll keep driving all night until your meter's worn out.'

'The chances are against it working,' he said.

'Are you telling me,' I told him. 'I'm in the business myself.'

'Okay, Buddy, just so you understand. Who do I report to?'

'Donald Lam,' I said. 'Just call up the apartment house and ask for me – and let's try and keep things so the clerk doesn't know what's happening. When this girl is ready to come down in the elevator, I'll phone the clerk to tell the cab-driver who is waiting at the desk that his services are no longer required. You can go out and put your car on a cruising basis.'

'Suppose she wants to hire me?'

'I think she has her own car, but if she wants to hire you that's easier than following.'

'Do I tell her the fare's been paid?'

'Definitely not. You collect from her and from me, too.'

'That,' he said, 'sounds more like it.'

He pocketed the twenty-dollar bill and I went back up

to the apartment. The clerk looked at me with speculative appraisal as I walked past the desk.

Up in the apartment Bernice Clinton said: 'I did, Donald.'

'What?'

'Go through your things. You haven't been living here long, have you?'

'No.'

'You look as though you were just living out of a suitcase.'

'Anything wrong with that?'

'For a bachelor, no. Where's your other place?'

'Who says I have any?'

She laughed and said: 'I'll bet you've got two or three places with a woman in each.'

'With expenses like that, I'd lease the corner lot for the first price anyone offered and fall all over myself doing it.'

'There's something mighty strange about you,' she said. 'I can't figure you out.'

'And I can't figure you out.'

She came walking over to me, put her hands behind my back, locked them around my waist, pressed herself up close to me, held her head back slightly so she could look in my eyes, and said: 'All right, Donald, what is it? Yes or no?'

'It's maybe.'

Abruptly her manner changed. She released her hands, stepped back, looked me over, said: 'When will you have an answer, Donald?'

'Whenever you've reached your top price.'

'I've reached it.'

'Including any bonuses?'

44

'Bonuses,' she said, 'don't go with the deal. If there are any bonuses, they're on a basis of friendship.'

'How do we get to be friends?'

'How do you usually get to be friends with those other girls? Tell me where your other apartment is.'

'I'm not keeping any woman or any women, if that's what you're referring to.'

'How about that good-looking babe that was with you last night?'

'I'm not keeping her.'

'No?'

'No.'

She said: 'All right. I'll tell you something about her, Donald. She's in love with you.'

I laughed and said: 'If you knew her better you'd know how preposterous that idea is.'

'I know her well enough,' she said, and then abruptly turning away, said: 'I'm going now. I'll give you a ring tomorrow.'

'Where?'

'Here at the apartment. Why? Is there any other place?'

'I might be in and out,' I said.

'If you're out, leave me a message. Either yes or no.'

'Will you boost the ante any?'

'No.'

'I'm inclined to accept.'

'That doesn't mean a thing,' she said. 'Inclinations are impulses. Impulses are transient. I'll give you a ring tomorrow.'

'Is there any place I can reach you?'

'Not now.'

'After we complete the deal?'

'Perhaps,' she said archly. 'I'm *inclined* to think so. It's an incipient impulse.'

I saw her to the door and telephoned the clerk, hoping to catch his ear while she was still in the elevator.

There was a second or two delay and I was on pins and needles, making a mental calculation. At length the clerk said: 'Hello.'

I said: 'Tell the cab-driver at the desk that I'm not going to need him. Is the elevator downstairs?'

'No, not yet. It's coming.'

'Never mind,' I said. 'Just tell the cab-driver where no one can hear you and don't mention names.'

'Very well,' he said, and hung up.

I settled down to twenty minutes of waiting. Then the phone rang.

I jumped for the receiver. 'Hello,' I said.

'This is your cab-driver. Your bird was wise.'

'What do you mean?'

'She came out just as I was leaving the lobby. She asked me if I was free, and I said I was now, that I'd been sent there on an order, but there was some mistake. The man must have given a wrong address. She stepped into the cab just as pert as you please and told me to take her to the Union Depot. You know how things are there at the depot. You bring your cab in at one place to discharge passengers. Then you have to circle around to another place to load.

'I brought her in and dropped her. She paid the cab fare. Then on a hunch I took a chance on getting pinched, just parked my cab and followed her into the depot.'

'What did she do?' I asked.

'Walked straight as an arrow out to the cab loading-place, stepped in another cab and drove away. I couldn't even get the number of the cab, and I couldn't possibly have followed her because the cab was out and on the street before I could get back and –'

'Any change out of that twenty?' I asked.

'Quite a bit.'

'Put it in your pocket and forget it,' I said. 'Only, tell me one thing: I was talking with the clerk on the telephone and he gave you my message. Now, was she in the lobby at that time?'

'No.'

'Was she in the lobby when you started out?'

'No, I was just about at the door when the elevator came down. It took a second for the doors to open. She did see me going out of the place. That's all.'

'Did she stop and talk with the clerk?'

'No. She breezed right on out the door, looked up and down the street, saw my cab, and asked me if I was vacant.'

'I don't get it,' I said.

'Neither do I,' he told me, 'but that's what happened.'

'Okay,' I said.

'I just might be able to dig up that other cab for you,' he said, 'the one that took her away. She's good-looking enough so that the cab-driver would have remembered her – no baggage or anything, coming out of the depot.'

'It would be a waste of time,' I said. 'You'd find she took that cab to one of the down-town hotels, walked into the lobby, walked out the other side and took another cab.'

'That Jane must be really covering her back trail,' he said.

'She's got it covered,' I told him. 'Pocket the change, have a good night's sleep and forget it.'

Chapter 6

Having determined that the telegram I had received had been filed at a branch office in the West End, I drove the agency heap out there around eleven o'clock the next morning.

A man was seated in the back, working a teletype. A good-looking young woman came up to the counter with a nice smile. 'May I help you?' she asked.

I showed her the message.

The welcoming smile faded from her face. Her expression became that of a poker player who encounters a raise.

'Well?' she asked.

'I received this message.'

'You're Donald Lam?'

'That's right.'

'Of the firm of Cool & Lam?'

'Yes.'

'Have you any identification?'

I showed her a driving licence.

'What did you want to know about the message?'

'Who sent it?'

She said: 'We try to keep an address of persons who send messages with signatures such as this, but we do this only so we will know what to do about delivering a reply in case there is one.'

48

'And do I get to see the name and address?' I asked.

'It wouldn't help.'

'Why?'

She said: 'After we had filed the message, I started checking and found there wasn't any such address, moreover there is no name in the city directory matching the one we had been given.'

'You're being very cagey and very cautious,' I said.

'We have rules, you know, Mr Lam.'

'Well,' I told her, 'I have problems. Perhaps we can make *your* rules fit *my* problems.'

She thought that over, gave me a quick glance, then averted her eyes.

'Do you *always* live according to rules?' I asked.

She looked back over her shoulder at the man at the teletype, then her eyes met mine. 'No,' she said.

'That's better,' I told her.

'How much better?'

'Lots better.'

'So where do we go from here?' she asked in a low voice.

'You can begin by telling me what made you suspicious about this telegram in the first place? Why did you look up the name and address?'

'It wasn't exactly suspicion,' she said, 'not at the start. It started out as curiosity.'

'Why?'

She was thoughtful for a moment, then glanced over her shoulder again.

She said: 'I have seen the young woman who sent that telegram before. She didn't remember me, but we've eaten several times at the same place.'

'Where?'

'A cafeteria about four blocks down the street.'

'Do you know her name?'

'No.'

'Can you describe her?'

Again she looked over her shoulder and said: 'I don't think I should be telling you these things, Mr Lam, and . . . well, people will wonder why I'm standing here talking so long.'

'There's only one "people" to worry about it.'

'Well, that's enough,' she said. 'He's the manager.'

'You eat lunch when?'

'At twelve-thirty.'

'I'll be waiting outside,' I said. 'We'll go to lunch down at the cafeteria. Perhaps you can point her out to me. In any event, you can describe her.'

I smiled and turned towards the door.

'Aren't you going to wait long enough for me to say yes or no?' she asked.

'If it's yes I don't need to wait,' I told her, 'and if it's no I don't want to hear it.'

I gave a quick glance back as I went out.

She was smiling. 'Wait half-way down the block,' she said.

I had some time to kill. I didn't want to go back to the agency, so I walked down to the cafeteria, looked the place over rather carefully, went to a phone-booth and let the telephone save me some leg work. Then I went back to the agency car, parked it down the street from the branch office of the telegraph company and waited.

She came out promptly at twelve-thirty.

I jumped out and opened the car door.

She got in, tucked her skirt around her leg and waited for me to close the door.

I closed the door, walked around, got in the driver's seat and said: 'You know my name. I don't know yours.'

'May,' she said.

'Just May?'

'My friends call me Maybe.'

I raised a quizzical eyebrow.

'That's for the middle initial, B, standing for Bernardine.'

'And the last name?'

'Maybe is enough,' she said, looking me over carefully.

'Why were you so cagey when I talked with you earlier?' I asked. 'Does that manager have it in for you?'

She laughed and said: 'It's a peculiar dog-in-the-manger attitude.'

'How come?'

'He's married, he has three children and he's in love with me.'

'Passes?' I asked.

'No,' she said. 'I could handle that in my stride. If he did that we'd have an understanding, get the atmosphere clarified and everything would be all right. But it doesn't come out in the open like that.'

'What does happen?'

'Nothing.'

'I don't get it.'

She said: 'I don't even know whether he knows he's in love with me or not; that is, consciously. I think his subconscious mind realizes it and his conscience bothers him because of that fact. So, instead of coming out in the open and being natural and spontaneous about it, he sits there and broods; and if he sees me being even courteous to some good-looking young man at the counter, he gets peeved and cranky— Good heavens,

51

you'd be surprised at the catechism I got just because I was talking with you.'

'What did you tell him?' I asked.

'What I tell him all the time,' she said. 'I make up stories that keep him satisfied and enable me to live with a situation that is becoming more and more intolerable.'

'What did you tell him?'

'I told him you were looking for a telegram that should have been sent to you and wasn't delivered and you were asking me questions about how incoming messages were handled where a person didn't have a street address and things of that sort.'

Again I glanced at her quizzically.

'I'm a graceful, gifted, accomplished liar,' she admitted airily, 'so don't look at me like that, Donald Lam. There are occasions when it's better to lie than to tell the truth, and when I encounter one of those occasions I'm most expert. . . . Now, there's a parking lot back of this cafeteria. You can run your car right in there and they'll stamp the parking ticket – Here we are, turn to the right.'

I went into the parking lot, parked the car and said: 'Now look, Maybe, there's a pretty good chance this young woman will know me when she sees me. I want to get someplace where I can be as inconspicuous as possible. I don't want to have her spot me if it can be avoided.

'I've looked the place over, and there are some tables up on the mezzanine floor. Those aren't quite as conspicuous as the ones downstairs.'

She said: 'I know. That's where the earnest couples meet when they want to engage in private conversations. Those tables are just for two and they're spaced so that there's a reasonable amount of privacy.'

'Can do?' I asked.

'Can do,' she said. 'It's fixed so you can go right up to the mezzanine and get your food from the counter up there if you want. They don't have quite the variety there as downstairs, but most of the same dishes that they have downstairs are up there.'

We entered the cafeteria, went upstairs, and as we started out with our trays towards the food the girl turned to me and said: 'Will you tell me something frankly, Donald?'

'Sure.'

'Are *you* buying my lunch?'

'I invited you, didn't I?'

'I mean, is it on an expense account or not?'

'It's on an expense account.'

'You're not paying for it individually?'

I shook my head.

'Then get ready for a shock,' she said. 'I'm going to have a double cut of rare roast beef. All I have for breakfast is black coffee and I'm famished by noon. My purse controls my appetite. Today, if you're sure you're on an expense account, I'm going hog-wild.'

'Go hog-wild,' I told her.

She did.

We sat down at one of the balcony tables which wasn't too prominent. The lights were dimmer up there, and we had a good view of the cashier's desk downstairs and the checking cashier at the end of the food line.

Maybe ate in a manner that showed she was a good healthy individual with a fine appetite and she was really enjoying the food.

'Don't they pay you enough so you can eat what you want?' I asked.

She smiled at me and said: 'Now you're probing into my personal affairs, Donald. The answer is yes, they pay me enough, but I have many uses for much money and I have to budget my income carefully.'

'Do you like the job there?'

'I love it. I love to watch people walk in and try to size them up to see what sort of a message they're going to send. Then I have an opportunity to check my conclusions when they bring the message to the counter.'

'How accurate can you guess?'

'Pretty darn accurate,' she said. 'I'm a good judge of character. For instance, down there at the checking desk, that woman who is just checking her tray is probably a married woman who has something on her mind. The man who is third back in the line is taking a very surreptitious interest in her. I have a feeling he's someone she's meeting surreptitiously. You watch. They'll get to the same table as though it happened by accident and it will be a table for two.'

'If that's the case, why didn't they come upstairs?' I asked.

'I don't know,' she said. Perhaps it's because it would look too intimate up here. . . . Now there she goes with her tray. You watch her. She'll pick out a table for two with a vacant chair.'

'Well, that part's all right,' I said. 'Any single un-attached woman would do the same thing and –'

'Now watch the man. He's just coming to the checker,' she said.

The man put up his tray on the checking desk, took the slip that the checker handed him and walked aimlessly around the room, looking for just the right place.

Finally he walked past the table where the woman was sitting, apparently without noticing the vacant chair, then having noticed it, turned, bowed politely and asked the woman, with elaborate impersonality, if anyone was sitting there.

She was very reserved, very dignified and frigidly polite. She apparently told him that the place was vacant. He thanked her and started unloading his tray.

'See what I mean?' she said.

'Now look,' I told her, 'either you're clairvoyant or you're making some kind of a grandstand that I can't fathom right now. I've been around a bit myself. It's my business to observe people. I never would have picked those two out as keeping a date.'

She said: 'I do things like that all the time, Donald.'

'The hell you do,' I told her. 'Now come down to earth and tell me. You can't pull that stuff with me and get away with it.'

She looked as though she might be going to cry. 'Donald,' she said, 'don't you trust me?'

'Hell, no,' I told her. 'Not when you pull stunts like that.'

She kept her eyes on her plate. 'I thought I was going to like you a lot – and now . . .'

I waited. When she said nothing I prompted her: 'And now?'

She looked up at me with an expression of righteous indignation. 'Now I don't know – I don't know if I even care to co-operate with you.'

She ate in hurt silence. I quit eating to watch her.

Abruptly she said: 'Donald, don't.'

'Don't what?'

'Don't look at me that way.'

'Don't try to pull fast ones like that on me, then,' I said.

'It wasn't a fast one, Donald.'

I looked over at the table where the couple she had picked out were seated. She was probably right about the marriage angle. The man was somewhere between forty-five and fifty and had kept his hair. There was an air of subdued sadness about him, the air of a man who had spent a long time looking for something, only to find out at last that it doesn't exist. There was just a little tired stoop about the shoulders. He was still slim, had kept his waistline as well as his hair and he wore his clothes with an air of distinction. The guy could be rich – and important.

From where I was sitting I couldn't get a very clear view of the woman. From time to time I could see her profile, but she had her back to me. Apparently, as nearly as I could judge from what I saw, she had a habit of using her eyes to advantage. She'd look away, then look up trustingly at her companion, smile and then lower her eyes. She could have been anywhere from twenty-six to thirty-one.

Sitting there looking at her, I wished I'd noticed her more when Maybe had first pointed her out. I was dimly aware of the fact that she had a rather good figure of a slender, streamlined type.

Then suddenly I saw Bernice Clinton. She was seated by herself at a corner table and her eyes were on the couple Maybe had pointed out to me.

Bernice's eyes were daggers ripping at the other woman's back, tearing the clothes off her to inventory everything that was underneath.

I hadn't seen Bernice when she came in, so I assumed she must have entered the cafeteria before we did.

Had she seen us?

She most certainly gave no indication that she had. Her eyes were on the couple, and from where she was seated she was in a position to see without being seen.

I looked over at Maybe.

'All right, sister,' I said. 'Come clean.'

'What do you mean, Donald?'

'You know damn well what I mean. You've seen those two together before.'

She lowered her eyes.

'That's how you knew they were going to sit down together. Come on now, who are they?'

'I – I don't know, Donald. I *have* seen them before, I admit that. I was trying to impress you, I guess.'

'You've seen them pull this same stunt of getting together?'

'Yes.'

'Is she the woman who sent me that telegram?'

'No. . . . The woman who sent the wire to you was more sexy, more of a – Donald, *there* she is!'

Maybe was looking down at Bernice Clinton.

'You mean the one sitting alone there and –'

'Yes, yes, that's the one! And she's looking at that couple. She's toying with her food and is just sitting there watching.'

'And she sent me the wire?'

'Yes. She's the one.'

'All this clairvoyant business of yours about that couple was a line?'

'Yes. I am blessed or cursed, whichever it is, with an unusual memory for faces and figures, Donald. I see a person once and somehow it seems that I never forget that individual. Every once in a while I'll see people on the street that I recognize as having been in the office to send telegrams, weeks or perhaps months earlier. I eat at this cafeteria regularly. Those two people have pulled that same stunt several times. They'll let other people get between them. Then the woman selects a table and the man comes along acting as though he's a perfect stranger. Then they gradually get acquainted and –'

'What happens when they go out?' I interrupted. 'Do they go out together?'

'No, the woman goes first. The man follows within a short time, but they keep up the fiction of being strangers who have simply engaged in a casual cafeteria conversation.'

I said: 'There's nothing casual about the way she's using her eyes on him.'

'I know, but . . . well, that's probably one of the reasons I noticed them. I saw the way she was using her eyes and, believe me, she certainly does put them to work – then when she got up and went out and paid her own check and left the man sitting there, I started wondering. Then a week or so later I saw them again, and then I saw them a couple of days ago, and this is the fourth time I've seen them here.'

I studied her for several seconds, then said: 'What's all this business of trying to impress me?'

'I – Donald, why do you suppose I let you take me out to lunch? Why do you suppose I . . . gave you a break?'

'Because you were hungry,' I said.

'No. Because I've seen you before and . . . you interested me.'

'When did you see me?'

'At the Masters' Grill on Seventh Street. You were having dinner with a heavy-set woman who seemed to be trying to dominate you, and who was thoroughly exasperated with you. She was old enough to be – Donald, *what* do you see in her?'

'You were looking at Bertha Cool, my business partner,' I said.

'So *that's* it!'

'That's it.'

'Does she love you?'

'Hell, no. She hates my guts.'

'She doesn't hate you, Donald. She's fond of you and she respects you. Down underneath she's a little afraid of you.'

'Could be,' I said indifferently.

She was watching me intently. 'Donald, if I've helped you, could you do something for me?'

'What?'

'Help me get a new job.'

'What's wrong with the one you have?'

'The manager.'

'Why don't you simply ask to be transferred?'

'I'm afraid to.'

'Why?'

'Well, it would hurt him terribly and . . . well, I don't know. I am afraid he'd try to prevent my leaving. I . . . I'm afraid of him.'

'He's really in love with you?'

'In a crazy, puritanical, frustrated sort of way he's in love with me.'

'All right,' I told her. 'I'll keep you in mind. I can't drive you back to work. I've got fish to fry.'

'I'll walk back to work,' she said. 'I took enough chances as it was, getting in your car so near the office. If he should happen to see us together . . . well, it would hurt him, and I don't like to hurt him.'

'Now look here, Maybe,' I said, 'let's cut out the play-acting for once. Are you going to live your whole life try-ing to keep from hurting the feelings of that manager?'

'No, that's why I want to get into something else.'

'What's your last name?'

'Hines. *H-i-n-e-s*,' she said.

'Why were you so cagey about it when I asked you?'

'I wanted to play you along, Donald. I wanted to get acquainted. I wanted to size you up. . . . I was worried about that big woman I'd seen you with. I wasn't sure about you at first.'

'Are you sure about me now?'

'I like you, Donald. I fell for you the minute you spoke to me. I guess you could tell it. The manager knew. He was furious.'

She glanced at her wrist-watch. 'I have to be back, Donald, right on the dot. I don't dare to be a single second late.'

'You've got plenty of time yet,' I said, 'time enough for me to ask you a few questions so I can see if you're playing square with me now.'

'I am, Donald. I swear it. What questions do you want to ask?'

'Just questions,' I said. 'Don't answer them if you don't want to, but if you do tell me anything, tell me the truth.'

'I will, Donald. I swear it.'

I held her eyes and said suddenly: 'This manager you're talking about, has he made passes at you?'

60

For a moment her eyes wavered, then they came back to mine. 'Yes.'

'Ever get to first base?'

'Yes.'

'You're afraid of him because of that?'

'Yes.'

'That's better,' I said.

'Oh, Donald, *why* did you make me tell you that? Donald, I . . . I – Donald, that wasn't fair, the way you got that out of me. If his wife knew . . .'

'If we're going to be friends,' I said, 'you're going to play ball with me.'

'Donald, I – Something about you frightens me.'

'That's good,' I told her.

'Why is it good?'

'It'll keep you truthful.'

'Donald, I've been . . . I've been devastatingly truthful. I – You sneaked up on my blind side. I . . .'

The woman who had been meeting the distinguished-looking man finished her luncheon, arose without so much as a glance at the man, and headed for the cashier's desk.

I said: 'This is where I leave you, Maybe.' I pushed back my chair, patted her shoulder and hurried down the stairs.

The cashier's desk was back out of Bernice's line of vision. I reached it just as the woman I was interested in was picking up her change.

I paid my check and reached the street in time to see her turn left, cross the street and keep on walking.

I followed along about thirty or forty feet behind. I didn't care whether she knew it or not.

She had quite a walk. It had a smooth sway. It wasn't

C

61

fast enough to be a wiggle. It had a seductive rhythm, as though the air were a swimming-pool and she was moving with perfectly timed strokes.

While she was walking along, a car passed us. It was an Olds being driven by the man who had been seated at the table in the cafeteria with her.

He gave no sign of recognition and she didn't even look his way.

I did a quick take on the licence number. It was JYJ 114.

My girl walked two blocks to a bus-stop. I got on the same bus she did and followed her up-town to an office building.

There was no use trying to cover up at this point. Either she knew me or she didn't. I didn't think she'd noticed me.

She entered the elevator and I got in the same elevator with her.

She looked me over and I looked her over. She said 'seven' to the operator, and then, as I said 'seven', she averted her eyes modestly as a woman is supposed to do when a man with wolfish tendencies meets her eyes in an elevator.

She got out at the seventh floor and walked down a long corridor. I walked along behind her. There had been no slightest sign of recognition when she looked at me in the elevator, but she knew I was following her. She could hear my steps in the corridor. She didn't look back.

There were double doors marked: HERBERT JASON DOWLING, and down below that: DOWLING LEASEHOLD APPRAISAL AND DEVELOPMENT COMPANY.

My girl went in there.

I walked in right behind her.

She smiled at the receptionist, opened the gate in the counter, went back into the reception office while I stood at a plaque marked: INFORMATION.

A young woman came over and smiled at me.

'Is Mr Dowling in?' I asked.

'Not at the moment,' she said. 'May I ask who's calling?'

My girl had started through a door to an inner office. Now she hesitated perceptibly, long enough to hear my name.

I raised my voice slightly. 'Donald Lam,' I said.

The girl I had been shadowing turned the knob and opened the door. Either my name meant less than nothing to her, or else she was a marvellous actress. I kept watching her out of the corner of my eye, but kept my face pointed towards the receptionist.

'What was the nature of your business, Mr Lam?' she asked.

'It's personal,' I said. 'Private, confidential. I'll call again.'

I turned and went out, took a bus back to the parking place, realized that I'd forgotten to get the cafeteria to stamp my parking ticket, knew that Bertha wouldn't sleep a wink that night if she'd realized it, paid thirty-five cents for parking charges, got in the car and drove to the apartment.

The clerk had a message for me. 'A young woman telephoned and asked if you'd left a message for a Miss B. C.,' he said.

'How did you know she was young?' I asked.

'Her voice,' he said, flushing slightly. 'She said she'd call again at five o'clock.'

I said: 'When she calls again tell her you delivered the message to me and that I left one for her.'

'Yes, Mr Lam,' he said, holding a pen poised over a memo pad. 'What's your message?'

'Tell her,' I said, 'that I'm willing to close, but that I don't know yet with whom I am going to close.'

That was all I needed at the apartment. I walked out and left him standing there, puzzled, his pen poised over the paper, his mouth open.

Chapter 7

I drove the agency car back down to the office building where Dowling had his offices, and then drove into a parking lot that was within half a block of the place.

'I'm thinking of getting offices near here,' I said. 'Do you have any regular parking stalls?'

'We can make one, but right now transient business is booming and it would be pretty expensive.'

'Where are your parking places for regular customers?' I asked.

'Over there against that wall – that's the choice place. You can get out through either exit. You just leave your car here and we'll park it.'

I walked over thoughtfully, studying the parking spaces.

'We aren't going to have any vacancies in this particular section that I know of, but the tenth space down is where we start parking transients. We could reserve a permanent space in that section.'

I was giving the parked cars the once-over. The Oldsmobile with the licence number JYJ 114 was in stall number five.

'Okay,' I said to the attendant, 'I'll let you know if I close the deal on the office in this building.'

I walked with him back to the entrance. He gave me a ticket on the agency car and parked it.

I was back in ten minutes. 'Forgot to get something out of the car,' I told him, showing him my ticket.

He started to say something as I walked in and then suddenly grinned and said: 'Oh yes. You're the one I was talking to about a monthly rental.'

'That's right,' I told him.

He consulted the parking ticket, then looked at a notation and said: 'You're in the third row back towards the rear. Can you find it all right?'

'Sure,' I told him.

I went back to the agency car and got out an electric bug, one of the newest devices for electronic shadowing. I always keep a set in the car.

I put in new batteries so as to be certain I'd have plenty of power, and on my way out walked over to the regular parking stalls and stood looking at them thoughtfully.

I waited until the parking attendant was busy with a customer, then slipped around the back of the car with licence number JYJ 114, attached the electronic bug to the rear bumper and walked out.

The attendant waved me on.

One of the hardest chores a detective has is hanging around on a city street, trying to make himself inconspicuous, keeping an eye on the entrance of an office building and waiting.

For the first fifteen or twenty minutes it's possible to be more or less interested in window displays, then in people passing by. After a while, however, a person's mind gets fed up and that magnifies all of the disagreeable physical symptoms which go with that sort of an assignment. You want to sit down. Your leg muscles and back muscles feel weary. You're conscious of the fact that your feet hurt, that the city pavements are hard.

I waited a solid two hours before my man came out of the office building. He came out alone.

I wasn't far behind him when he entered the parking lot and hurried over to his car.

The attendant recognized me once more and said: 'What did you do about that office?'

'I haven't made up my mind yet,' I said. 'It's a sublease. I have a couple of them I'm figuring on; one here and one that's out quite a ways where there's usually kerb parking.'

'That kerb parking is undependable and annoying, particularly when it rains,' he said.

I kept trying to get him to take my money. 'Okay,' I told him. 'I'm in a rush right now. I know where the car is. Want me to drive it out?'

'I'll have one of the boys get it,' he said. 'It's one of the rules on transients. Regulars drive out their own cars.'

'Make it as snappy as you can, will you?' I asked.

'Oh, that's all right,' he said. 'You're going to be a regular. You'll get in the office building here. You don't want to lease a place way out in the sticks. You get business where the business is, not where it isn't.'

I grinned at him, handed him a couple of dollars and said: 'By the time you get the parking charge figured up, there should be a cigar in it for you.'

I hurried over to the agency heap, jumped in, started the motor and was just in time to see the car I wanted to shadow turn to the left.

I was held up a bit trying to make a left turn. By the

time I'd made it he was gone. Traffic was pretty heavy.

I turned on the electric bug, and the signal came in loud and clear.

I made time and picked him up within ten blocks. I stayed half a block behind him, letting lots of cars keep in between us, listening to the steady beep . . . beep . . . beep.

After fifteen minutes of traffic driving he turned to the left. I couldn't see him, but the electric bugging device gave steady beeps when it was straight ahead, short half-beeps when the car I was following was to the left, and long drawn-out beeps when it turned to the right. If it ever got behind me, the beep turned to a buzz.

I turned left too soon and got a signal showing that I was still behind him, but he was to the right. After a while the signal became a buzz and I knew he was behind me. That meant he'd probably parked someplace. I made a big circle until I located the car parked at the kerb in front of an apartment house.

I found a parking place half a block away, sat in the car and waited.

My quarry was in the apartment house for two hours. Then he came out and started driving towards the beach.

By this time it was dark. I could get up close to him where there was traffic, but had to drop far behind when there wasn't traffic. My lights would have been a give-away if I'd tried to shadow him in the conventional manner. Moreover, I'd have lost him if it hadn't been for the electronic shadowing device. . . . His signal was coming loud and clear, and then all of a sudden it turned to a buzz. I circled the block and found he was in the parking lot of a high-class restaurant.

I sat where I could watch the exit and realized I was

hungry. I sat there with the faint odour of charcoal-broiled steaks tantalizing my nostrils and occasionally catching the aroma of coffee.

My man came out an hour later, drove to the beach, turned right, and after half a mile went to the Swim and Tan Motel.

It was a fairly modern motel, with quite a bit of electrical display in front. I remembered it was the Peeping Tom place.

I waited until my man was coming out of the office with the key to a cabin before I went in to register.

The card the man I was shadowing had filled out was still on the counter. I noticed that he was in Unit 12 and that he had registered under the name of Oscar L. Palmer and wife, giving a San Francisco address.

He had written out the licence number of his car, but had transposed the last two figures, an old dodge which is still good. Ninety-nine times out of a hundred the motel manager doesn't check the licence number on the plates against the licence number the tenant writes out. If he does, it's still better than an even chance he won't notice the transposition of the numbers, and if he should notice it, the thing can be passed off as an honest mistake.

I used the alias of Robert C. Richards, gave the first three letters and the first and last figure of the licence number on the agency heap, but a couple of phony numbers in between.

I could have written anything. The manager of the motel was a woman who apparently didn't care. She was complying with the law in regard to registrations, but she certainly wasn't checking licence numbers or bothering the tenants.

'You mean you're all alone, Mr Richards?'

'That's right.'

'Your wife isn't going to join you – later?'

'I don't think so.'

'If you expect her to show up,' she said, 'you'd better put "and wife" on there. It's a formality, you know.'

'Any difference in the rate?' I asked.

'Not to you,' she said, smiling. 'It's ten dollars either way. There are ice-cubes in a container at the far end and in another by the office. There are three soft-drink vending machines, and if you should be joined by – anybody – try to keep things quiet, if you will. We like to run a nice quiet place.'

'Thank you,' I told her.

I took another sidelong glance at the other registration card, then took the key to Unit 13 that she had given me and went down long enough to park the car.

The construction was reasonably solid; not like the cracker-box construction of so many of the motel units that have stucco all over the outside, but walls that are thin enough so you can hear every movement of the people in the adjoining apartment.

I put a small electric amplifier against the wall on the side I wanted to case. With the aid of that I could hear my man moving around, heard him cough a couple of times, heard the toilet flush, heard the sound of water running.

Whoever his companion was going to be, she was going to join him later. She knew where to come. He didn't have to telephone.

I was so hungry my stomach felt all lines of communication had been severed. It's one thing to go without food when you're occupied with some work or when you're simply postponing a meal, but when you're dependent on someone else and know that you *can't* eat until he's bedded down for the night, hunger can be a gnawing torture.

I had noticed a drive-in down the road a quarter of a mile. The batteries on the bugging device I had put on the car were still fresh enough to send out good strong signals. The powerful microphone I could press against the wall between my motel unit and that occupied by the man would bring in the sound of any conversation, and I was positively nauseated I was so hungry.

I got in the car, drove down to the drive-in and ordered a couple of hamburgers with everything included, a cup of coffee and the fastest service possible.

The place wasn't particularly busy at that time of night, and the girl who was waiting on me, who was clothed in the tightest-fitting pair of slacks I had ever seen on a woman and a sweater that showed everything there was – and there was lots of it – wanted to be sociable.

'You really in a hurry, Handsome?' she asked.

'I'm in a hurry, Beautiful.'

'It's early in the evening to be in a hurry. There's lots of time left.'

'There may not be any women left,' I said.

She gave a little pout and said: '*I* don't get off work until eleven o'clock. That's when my evening commences.'

'I'll be here at ten-fifty-five,' I said.

'Oh, *you!*' she announced. 'That's what they all say. What's that thing going buzz-buzz-buzz in your car?'

I said: 'Darn it, that's the automatic signal that shows when the ignition key is on. I didn't turn it off.' I reached over and switched off the electronic bugging device.

She went in to get the hamburgers, and I switched on the device again and kept the signal from Dowling's car coming in steady and clear until I saw her starting back with the hamburgers. Then I shut off the device again.

She wanted to hang around while I was eating. 'Don't you think it's selfish to have dinner *before* you go to pick her up?'

'No,' I said. 'It's a kindness to her. You see, she's on a diet. She'll eat just a pineapple and cottage cheese salad and I'm to have one with her so she won't feel out of place.'

'Diets can be terrible,' the girl said. 'How much overweight is she?'

'Not a bit,' I said, 'but she's keeping her figure in hand.'

She looked at me provocatively. 'Good figures *should* be kept in hand,' she said, and walked away with an exaggerated wiggle.

I turned on the device again, half fearful that I might find silence, but the buzzes came in loud and clear.

When I switched on the lights for her to come and get the check, I had the exact change plus a dollar tip.

'Look, Handsome,' she said, 'were you kidding about being back at ten-fifty-five?'

'I'm serious,' I told her.

'Well,' she said, 'we're not supposed to date customers but –'

'But it won't be ten-fifty-five tonight,' I said, 'it will be ten-fifty-five next week.'

For a moment her eyes flashed with anger. Then she laughed and said: 'All right, Smarty-pants. Just for that I'll be difficult.'

She picked up the money, then suddenly smiled. 'Thanks for the tip, Handsome.'

'Thanks for the service, Beautiful.'

'It's a pleasure,' she said. 'You really are cute. What's your name?'

'Donald.'

'Mine's Debby. I'll see you – next week, ten-fifty-five. Don't forget.'

'I won't,' I told her, and drove away.

The buzzes turned to beeps as I swung the car around, and the signals were coming in satisfactorily.

It was just as I was turning in at the entrance of the motel that I met another car coming out. My headlights for one fleeting moment glared in the face of the other driver. I had to slam on my brakes to keep her from hitting me. She was coming out of the place so fast her tyres screamed as she turned on to the pavement.

I had that one brilliantly illuminated flash of her features. It was like seeing someone by the light given by a flash of lightning. I only saw her for half a second but her face was etched in my mind. The features were those of a woman who had sustained an emotional shock.

There was no reason on earth to connect her with the man I was shadowing, but the expression of frozen horror on her face, the way she was driving the car, made me decide to risk a gamble.

I backed my car around and took after her. She was driving a Chevy two years old. I had to floor-board the throttle. She went through the first traffic signal on red but did stop for the next red signal. That gave me a chance to catch up so I could get the licence number on her car. It was RTD 671.

That was all the gamble I dared to make. I turned around and headed back for the motel.

I parked my car in front of Unit 13, got out my key, went inside, locked the door, took the electronic listening device from my brief-case, put the microphone up against the wall and waited for sounds.

There weren't any.

I moved the control which put the device up to its highest potential. There were still no sounds.

I wondered if the batteries were dead. I got out fresh batteries, put them in and again put the device up against the wall.

Still no sound.

I moved over to the wall on the other side and tried Unit 14.

The device worked perfectly. The couple in 14 were in bed and whispering. I could hear every word they were whispering, hear their breathing in between whispers.

I went back to the wall between my unit and 12 and tried it again.

Absolute, complete silence. I couldn't hear any breathing.

If my man had gone out, he had left his car parked in front. I had let my stomach dictate to my brain and now I was kicking myself. I had shadowed a car. The car was still there but the man I wanted had gone.

There was one other possibility.

I took a pitcher and went out to the box containing the ice-cubes. I found I could get to the back of the motel units through a little passageway.

This motel was a perfect set-up for a Peeping Tom. The units were rectangular, but the bath and toilet in the back converted the interior into an L-shaped space.

The narrow part behind the bath had been made into a little breakfast nook with a table and benches. There was a window in this nook which gave cross-ventilation to the room, but the shade couldn't be pulled down except by reaching all the way across the table.

Since the window faced the black vacancy at the end of the lot, no one seemed to bother to pull the shades on those windows.

I saw lighted oblongs in several of the units as I moved cautiously over to Unit 12.

My man had pulled the shade a little but not all the way. There was a lighted crack between the edge of the window and the shade.

I moved closer and put my eye against the crack. I could see a foot on the floor, covered with a shoe that was on its side. I could see a couple of inches of woven sock over the man's ankle.

I couldn't see anything else.

I looked hastily up and down the passageway. To be caught as a Peeping Tom in this particular motel could be damn embarrassing. I'd be tagged with all the other complaints. However, I was interested in that foot. I applied my eye to the crack in the window once again.

The foot was still there, in the same position as before. But this time I saw something else – a thin trickle of dark red, and, as I looked, the trickle moved perhaps another sixteenth of an inch along the floor.

Then I saw something else. The window had a bullet hole in it, but there was no bullet hole in the shade. That meant a bullet had gone through the window and *after* that *someone* on the *inside* had pulled the shade nearly all the way down.

I started back for my cabin but had to go on around Unit 14 to get to the box containing the ice-cubes.

A woman was just emerging from the shower in Unit 14. She was a living doll with a figure that would have delighted an artist.

I slowed down slightly. I could no more help looking than a compass needle could help pointing north.

The stream of light hit me. She must have felt my eyes. She looked up. She didn't scream or try to cover up. She simply moved with calm efficiency over towards the part of the room where I knew the telephone would be.

I sprinted around the end of the place, grabbed my brief-case with the electric microphone, closed the door, jumped in the agency car, started the motor and backed into a turn.

I was midway in the block when the police car went whizzing past me, headed towards the Swim and Tan Motel.

It was that close.

It wasn't until then that the significance of the steady buzzing which was growing constantly fainter dawned on me and made me realize my predicament.

The Oldsmobile parked at the motel was now behind me. The electric buzzer was sending out its automatic signals.

And when the police checked the car of the murdered man, they'd find my electric bug clamped to his rear bumper.

Chapter 8

I got busy on the phone and chased down licence numbers.

The Olds with licence number JYJ 114 was registered to Herbert J. Dowling.

That was no surprise.

The Chevy licence number RTD 671 was registered to Irene Addis and the address was Apartment 643, 3064 Deane Drive. In this business you soon learn that you can't argue with facts so I didn't try.

I headed the agency car for Deane Drive. The address turned out to be a pretty fair-looking apartment house, and the street door was unlocked. There was no one on duty in the lobby. I went up to Apartment 643 and pressed the mother-of-pearl button which caused chimes to sound in the interior.

After the second sound of the chimes the door was opened. The frozen-faced young woman I had glimpsed briefly in the car said: 'Good evening . . . I'm sorry, you must have the wrong apartment.'

I shook my head. 'No, I have the right place. I want to talk to you.'

Despite the frozen face she wasn't bad-looking: clean-cut regular features, steady blue eyes, chestnut hair and a rather slim chassis with curves that could have been emphasized a bit more without hurting her appearance, but she wasn't flat-chested or bean pole. She was all woman.

She said: 'I'm sorry but I don't know you and —'

'You almost ran into me at the Swim and Tan Motel,' I said. 'You were leaving there – in a hurry – as I drove in.'

'I have never been at the Swim and Tan Motel in my life!' she snapped.

'Do we discuss it here or inside?' I inquired.

'Neither! I don't know what you— Oh, you must be the driver who . . .' She cut off the speech, trying to call back the words as they left her mouth.

I grinned at her confusion.

'Come in,' she invited and opened the door.

I went in and kicked the door closed behind me.

'There may not be much time,' I said. 'Tell me about you and Dowling.'

'How *dare* you —'

'Save in,' I interrupted. 'You haven't time for an act. You've got to get right down to brass tacks.'

'Who . . . who *are* you?'

'I could perhaps help you, but in any event I have to know the facts *fast*.'

'Why should I tell *you* anything?'

'Why not? The police will be here any minute and I could give you a good dress rehearsal.'

'Just who are you?'

'You can call me Donald. I'm a detective.'

'Then . . . you're with the police!'

'Not me. I'm a private detective. I want the facts.'

'I have nothing to say to you.'

'Okay,' I told her. 'The police will give me all the

breaks I need in return for the information I can give them.'

I walked over to the phone.

She watched me, then abruptly caved in. 'Don't, Donald! *Please* don't. I'll tell – I'll do anything you want. I *can't* afford to have the police asking questions, and . . . all the publicity. I'd kill myself first.'

I said: 'I'll give you a chance to come clean, but it has to be all the way, Irene. Don't try to hold back anything or you'll find it's the most expensive mistake you ever made.'

'I want to – I have to tell someone,' she said.

'Start with Dowling,' I said.

'Was that his name?' she asked. 'I never knew his identity. I was –'

'Quit lying,' I told her.

'I'm not lying. I had no idea . . .'

I picked up the telephone, dialled the number 9. From where she was standing it looked as though I was dialling Operator.

I said into the telephone: 'Operator, will you get me police headquarters, please. This is Donald Lam, a detective, and I want to report a homicide and a witness who –'

She was all over me in a fury of panic, wrenching the telephone out of my hands, slamming it down into its cradle.

'No!' she said. 'No . . . no, you mustn't!'

She began to cry.

I said: 'I told you once that acting wouldn't do you any good and you're wasting a lot of valuable time.'

'What . . . what do you want to know?'

'What you were doing down at the motel, what you know about Dowling's death and how long your affair with him has been going on.'

'I wasn't having any affair. I –'

'I know, I know,' I said. 'You'd *like* to lie out of it. You think that if you turn your back on it, it will go away. It isn't going to go away. This is murder. Murders don't just walk off and unhappen just because you want them to. I'm giving you a chance to rehearse your answers before the police arrive and it's a wonderful break for you.'

'I'm answering your questions,' she said.

'Answer them right, then,' I told her. 'If you keep on the way you're starting, you'll be in a cell, charged with murder, by midnight. You'll know what it's like to have newspaper reporters standing around scribbling down what you have to say, photographers with flashlights begging you to give them just a little more cheesecake and look sexy, because it's going to be that kind of a case. You can see the headlines, "MILLIONAIRE MURDERED IN LOVE NEST BY JILTED MISTRESS." '

'I wasn't his mistress and I wasn't jilted.'

'I know,' I said. 'You went down there to discuss an option on a mining property you own.'

'I tell you I wasn't his mistress. I went down there – It was a business proposition.'

'Sure,' I told her. 'You had two shares of stock in Dowling's company and he wanted to get the voting rights on it. You knew there was a fight for control coming up at the next stockholders' meeting. So he told you where he'd be and suggested you join him, using the name of Mrs Oscar L. Palmer. You could spend the night talking it over without being interrupted. That would help you make up your mind what you wanted to do with your proxy.'

'You're terrible,' she said. 'You're a mean, nasty-minded . . .'

'Go on,' I told her, as she hesitated. 'Remember, you're rehearsing your answers for the police. This sort of answer isn't going to get you anywhere except into a cell; but if you like to put on an act, go ahead.'

'How do you know I was to meet him at the motel?'

'Because you were leaking secrets from the Carson Associates Securities Investment Pool. Dowling was getting confidential information from you, capitalizing on it and –'

'But that's absurd!'

'What's absurd about it? By the time they check into Dowling's affairs they'll find out that's *exactly* what was happening. When they get into his private office, they'll find a lot of information about what investments Carson was making and what investments he intended to make. It will turn out to be highly confidential information which must have been furnished by some one of Carson's employees who was on the inside.

'Then the police find out that you were posing as Mrs Palmer, that Dowling was registered as Oscar L. Palmer.

'Then they'll check into your past, find out when you first met Herbert Dowling and –'

'No!' she exclaimed. 'No! No!'

'That bothers you?' I asked.

She said: 'That – Oh my God, will they do that?'

'What?'

'Check into my past and when I first knew Dowling?'

'Sure,' I said.

She said: 'Look, Mr Lam, I –'

'Better call me Donald,' I said. 'We're going to see a lot more of each other in the next half-hour or so before the police get here – if it's that long.'

'All right, Donald, then. I wasn't Herbert Dowling's mistress. That is, I mean, it had been a long while ago. I *didn't* go down there to join him as his wife . . . his mistress.'

I started an elaborate yawn.

'Mr Dowling,' she said with dignity, 'is the father of my child.'

I snapped the yawn off in the middle and sat bolt upright in the chair.

'What?'

'That's right,' she said. 'I have a three-year-old boy in a private home.'

'And Dowling was the father?'

'Yes.'

'Did he admit it?'

'I don't know what you mean by admitting it. He never tried to deny it, at least with me.'

'How is the child supported?'

'He supports him.'

'You mean he pays for the boy's support?'

'Certainly. He sees that I have money to deposit in my account on the first of each and every month covering our son's expenses for the following month.'

'All right,' I told her, 'this is important. How did that money get into your account?'

'Through deposits.'

'I know, I know. But how were the deposits made? Who signed the cheques?'

'The cheques,' she said, 'were invariably cashier's

cheques. They were made out in the names of different persons and properly endorsed and presented to the bank to be deposited to my account. Because they were cashier's cheques, and because the person who presented them didn't want to draw money but simply to make a deposit, the bank accepted the cheques without question and deposited same to my account. The bank may have been a little curious but never gave any evidence of that curiosity.'

'And you checked this money out on the boy's expenses?'

'Yes.'

'In your own name?'

'In my own name,' she said. 'The boy thinks his father was killed in an automobile accident. I have built up an elaborate background of ficton.'

'Good Lord,' I told her, 'you left a back trail that anyone and everyone can follow.'

'How did I know it was going to be a back trail?' she said.

'All right,' I said. 'Let's get down to brass tacks. I want to know all the background.'

'I want to explain certain things first.'

'Never mind the explanation,' I said, 'give me all the facts. The explanations can come later.'

'If you don't have the explanations, the whole thing sounds sordid.'

I said: 'You have a child born out of wedlock and you don't want people to think there's anything wrong about it. Is that right?'

'That's exactly right,' she flared. 'How many people in the world live the orthodox lives they're supposed to? How many people conform to the standards that are set up by the moralists? There are certain rules that just don't work when you come down to real life.'

'Go on,' I said. 'Let's have it. Let's have all of it.'

She said: 'I worked for Mr Dowling. He was attracted to me and I was attracted to him. I sympathized with him.'

'Why?'

'His wife had heart trouble. She couldn't have any emotional strain – no strain of any sort. She wasn't a wife, she was just a woman. She wasn't even a woman, she was a patient, a cardiac cripple. Dowling had to handle her with kid gloves. He couldn't cross her in anything, he couldn't give her anything to worry about, and he couldn't have any normal man-and-wife companionship.'

'So he sought that with you.'

'It wasn't like that, Donald. Don't make it sound so sordid when it wasn't. It was a beautiful thing – while it lasted.'

'What stopped it?' I asked.

'My pregnancy.'

'Why did that stop it?'

'He was afraid she'd find out about it and that would have killed her. If she had had any idea of the affair, it would have killed her. She was hanging on to life by a thread and he was *so* loyal to her, so devoted and so . . . . so intensely generous and human that he would have sacrificed everything to protect her.'

'You mean he was so generous that he sacrificed you.'

'Put it that way if you want, but I wouldn't have had it any other way. He couldn't have tried to get a divorce. That would have killed her. If she'd found out about what was going on, that would have been terribly

BACHELORS GET LONELY

upsetting and if she had found out that there was a baby involved, it would have been fatal. He knew it and I knew it. It was one of the chances we had to take.'

'So what?'

'So I went away.'

'He furnished the money?'

'He furnished the money and I had to be away for nearly a year. When I came back . . . well, of course, I'd been away and he was an intensely lonely man . . .'

'And your place had been taken by another,' I said.

'He had found other interests.'

'And his wife had died?'

'She died two weeks before I came back.'

'So what?'

'I wouldn't beg, I wouldn't whimper, I wouldn't try to use any hold over him. I simply went out, got another job and never saw him except at very rare intervals when I had to consult him about something that affected Herbert's life.'

'You called your son Herbert?'

'He wanted me to.'

'Any family resemblance?' I asked.

'He's the spitting image of his father and he gets to look more like him every day of his life.'

'Does Dowling ever see him?'

'Yes, that's the point. He thinks Mr Dowling is his uncle. Mr Dowling saw him a few times, but the resemblance is so pronounced, so startling that . . . well, Mr Dowling is a prominent man and if there should be a scandal at this particular time it might very well ruin him.'

'I suppose he told you that if you'd just have the child

85

and hang on until after his wife died, he would marry you.'

'That's what he intended to do at the time.'

'And he changed his mind?'

'He changed his mind.'

'And now wouldn't consider marriage?'

'On the contrary,' she said, 'he asked me several times to marry him and I refused.'

'Why?'

'Because I think he would be actuated more by a sense of duty than by a sense of love.'

'You have your son to consider.'

'I know it. Things can't go on like this. I – Well, that was one of the things I wanted to talk to him about.'

'And he agreed to meet you?'

'Yes.'

'And he was planning to renew the affair?'

'Certainly not,' she said. 'There's nothing like that between us now.'

'But he registered as husband and wife.'

'Of course he did. You can't go to a high-class motel and have a woman come and visit you without making at least *some* concession to the conventions – and that was particularly true right at the moment because Mr Dowling is under heavy pressure from some of the disgruntled stockholders who would like to wrest control of the corporation from him.'

'Why didn't you meet somewhere and drive into the motel together?'

'That's what he intended to do but I was delayed. I had to telephone him at the restaurant where I was to join him and tell him that he'd have to go on down to the motel and register and I'd come in later.'

'So you came in later?'

'Yes.'

'And then what happened?'

'He was dead.'

'You're sure?'

'I'm sure. I – Oh, Donald, it was terrible.'

'All right, what happened?'

'I thank my lucky stars,' she said, 'that I didn't stop at the office the way I intended to and tell them that I was Mrs Palmer and ask if my husband had registered yet, because we were to meet, and –'

'That gambit is supposed to fool a motel manager?' I asked.

'Certainly not,' she said, 'but it gives the manager an opportunity to size up the persons involved and know that they're not the brawling type and – Well, most of them don't care, just so you're decent and orderly.'

'But you didn't contact the manager?'

'No. I saw Mr Dowling's car parked in front of Unit Number 12, so I parked my car right alongside his and went up and tried the door.'

'You didn't knock?'

'Certainly not. That would be a give-away. I was supposed to be his wife. I was to walk up, open the door and walk right in, just as though I belonged there. '

'And the door was unlocked?'

'Yes. He had left it unlocked. That was the way we arranged things.'

'You opened the door and walked in?'

'Yes.'

'And then what?'

'He was lying on his side on the floor. He'd been shot.'

'How do you know it was a shot?'

'There was a – Oh, Donald, I can't . . . I just can't go on.'

She started to cry.

I said: 'Save the tears, Sister. This much I have to know. How do you know he was shot?'

'There was . . . there was a spot of blood, a . . . a bullet hole in the back window. I ran forward and bent over him. I touched his hand and the minute I did I knew he was dead. Of course, I felt certain he was dead when I saw his face.'

'The light was on in there?'

'Yes.'

'No other clues? Nothing to indicate who had been in there before you?'

'I didn't look. I just felt that terrific shock, that awful sense of loss and . . . well, I bent over him and felt his wrist and then I was overcome with panic.'

'Why?'

'I'm thinking of my boy. I can't have him involved in a scandal. He's going to grow up to be a good, well-behaved boy. He will orient himself with his surroundings, he will have friends, be accepted; everyone will think he's an unfortunate whose father was killed in an automobile accident.

'Now if it should turn out that he is illegitimate, that his father was murdered – Oh, Donald, it would mark him for life. He'd be ostracized by his companions, he'd be singled out for derision and contempt and – Children can be cruel. They can be little monsters.'

'Let's go back to the motel. What did you do?'

'I couldn't leave him there like that. I pulled the shade down on the back window. That seemed to give him a certain privacy – kept anyone behind the cabin from staring in and seeing him.'

I watched her thoughtfully. 'It also kept anyone behind the cabin from looking in and seeing you bending over a corpse and searching the body.'

'Donald, I didn't search the body.'

'But you did bend over him?'

'Yes.'

'After you pulled the shade?'

'Before.'

'There's no way you can prove it was before?'

'No – only my word for it.'

'Then what did you do?'

'I . . . I just gave one wild look around and then left the place, backed my car around and went tearing out of the driveway.'

'Did anybody see you?'

'There was a car driving in just as I was coming out. The headlights were full on my face for a minute. I suppose that you were the one driving that car.'

'Yes,' I said. 'That was when I saw you.'

'You drove on in?'

'Not all the way in. I turned around and followed you.'

'What was your interest in . . . in what was going on at the motel?'

'I was shadowing Dowling.'

'Oh,' she said in a weak, frightened little voice. 'Then you – Donald, you were employed by someone to shadow Mr Dowling?'

'Well, not exactly that, but I was employed to do certain things and in order to do them I thought I should shadow Dowling.'

'How long have you been shadowing him?'

'Just tonight.'

'Then you probably know that he's exceedingly . . . well, he's miserable. He's involved emotionally with a woman who just won't let him off the hook. He drifted into this alliance during my absence and now . . . now he's hooked.'

'What's her hold on him?' I asked.

'You mean the woman with whom he became involved?'

'Yes.'

'She's a demon, attractive, ruthless, savage. She has copies of hotel registrations, letters, tape-recordings made with concealed microphones. They crossed into Mexico several times and he took her on some trips where they crossed state lines.'

'Blackmail?'

'A highly refined form of blackmail,' she said. 'You see, he is – was – in a position where he simply couldn't afford to have anything happen that would jeopardize his reputation or undermine him with the stockholders of his company. I don't know whether you know it or not, but he's engaged in a fight to keep control of the company. Some rival business interests are trying to undermine the confidence the stockholders have in him so they can take over.'

'Do you know who those rival business interests are?' I asked.

'He's been so very, very careful not to tell me that I've sometimes wondered if . . .'

'Go on,' I said.

'If it isn't Mr Carson, the man I'm working for.'

'Would Carson do a thing like that?' I asked.

'Business is business,' she said.

'But you don't know it's Carson?'

'No, I don't know.'

'You and Dowling have evidently met several times and he's discussed his personal affairs with you in some detail.'

'He likes to confide in me,' she said. 'I think it was the big tragedy of his life when I had to leave and he was left a lonely man without any feminine companionship. He told me one time that after I left he wouldn't even look at a woman for weeks and then . . . well, he's intensely masculine and . . . well, the inevitable happened. This woman was very smart. He was very lonely. She sized up the situation and caught him unaware, got her hooks into him.

'It's hard to describe a man like that, Donald. He's emotionally restless. He's – Well, I always felt that we had a perfect companionship and that much of his present trouble is he had been searching for something to take the place of that companionship.'

'All right,' I said. 'He became emotionally involved. This woman got her hooks in him good.'

She nodded.

'Who is it?'

'I don't like to mention names. I can't violate his confidence.'

'Grow up,' I told her. 'The guy's dead.'

That statement hit her right between the eyes. In talking about Dowling she had become absorbed in what she was saying and for the moment had forgotten that he was dead.

She caught her breath. The tears came to her eyes.

'Forget it,' I said. 'You haven't time to be sorry. Who is this woman with whom he became emotionally involved?'

'Her name is Bernice Clinton.'

I thought that over.

'Know where she lives?' I asked.

'No. He never told me that, but I know that he kept her. He maintained an apartment for her and she had extravagant tastes.'

'And then he quit maintaining the apartment?'

'No, he still maintains it, but he desperately wants to get out from under.'

'Why?'

'Why does any man become involved in the first place if he's going to want to escape later?' she said. 'It's some kind of an emotional chemistry. He didn't see her the way she really is. He saw the reflection of my image in her. She led him on. He was completely infatuated with her for a while and then –'

'Why didn't he marry her when he became infatuated with her and after his wife had died?'

'Because he began to find out her real character.'

'And then Dowling wanted to resume the old relationship with you?'

'He wanted me,' she said. 'I couldn't go back the way he wanted. I respected him as the father of my child but somehow when I came back and found that he had become involved with that other woman, I . . . I don't know how to explain it, Donald. Something went dead inside of me. I just regarded him as a friend. I sympathized with him. I understood him, I think perhaps better than any woman has ever understood him. I liked him. But the idea of becoming involved emotionally . . .

well, I just couldn't take it. I've gone through all that once.

'If he had been free to marry me when I first came back, I'd have married him in a minute, but he had become involved and it was the same story all over again. I didn't want to go through the surreptitious meetings, the deceit, the clandestine affair and . . . and possibly another pregnancy.

'It's hard to explain how I felt towards him and it's difficult to explain how he felt towards me.'

'Did he try to make passes?'

'Yes – of course.'

'What do you mean, of course?'

'He's emotional. He's very much of a man and he liked me a lot and of course we had our background of intimacy and naturally it was only human nature that he wanted to resume.'

'You wouldn't let him?'

'No. I gave him my friendship, my sympathy, my understanding, but . . . I couldn't have any more clandestine intimacies. I couldn't take the chance of having another child tainted with the stigma of illegitimacy.'

'In other words, you told him he'd have to get rid of Bernice, be free to marry you and then lead you to the altar before you'd resume your old relationship?'

'I suppose it boiled down to something like that, yes.'

'What a perfect pigeon you are for a murder rap!' I said.

'You think they'll –?'

'Sure they will.'

I sat for an interval looking at her, thinking the situation over, sizing her up.

For some time she bore my scrutiny with outward

equanimity. Then she said suddenly: 'All right, Donald. I've been mentally undressed by men. This is a new experience. You're mentally dissecting me. Quit it.'

I said: 'I have to know what makes you tick. I'm gambling that it's your son.'

'There's no gamble,' she said. 'It *is* my son. I'm living my life for him.'

'That's the way I figure it,' I told her. 'Otherwise you'd have been involved in other affairs. You'd have resumed where you left off with Dowling. Once you became a mother you started working at it.'

'And why do we discuss all this at the present time?' she asked.

'Because,' I told her, 'I'm going to give you some advice and you're going to follow it.'

'What's the advice?'

'You're in a spot,' I said. 'If you go to the police now and tell them your story, you become involved. You make the front pages of the newspapers. Your son comes into the limelight.'

Her eyes showed dark panic. 'No, Donald, no,' she pleaded.

'If,' I said, 'you *don't* go to the police, then you are playing into their hands. They have an opportunity to find out who was to occupy Unit 12 at the Swim and Tan Motel under the name of Mrs Oscar L. Palmer.

'The police will do two things. First, they'll search the premises for evidence. Second, they'll start trying to find the woman who was to meet Dowling at the motel.'

She nodded.

I said: 'If you leave here abruptly, that means you have resorted to flight, and flight is an evidence of guilt.

94

It can be introduced in evidence as a big factor in a murder case.'

'Donald, what are you trying to do, drive me crazy?'

'No,' I said. 'I'm trying to show you why you have to follow my advice.'

'But you can't give me any advice that will help,' she said. 'You've just analysed the situation to show that I'm in such a spot I can't move. I've got to stay here paralysed until the searching spotlight of the police investigation discloses me to the public and then – then my son's life is ruined.'

I said: 'Get this straight, Irene. Sooner or later your son is going to have to enter into the picture. But it makes a great difference whether he has to enter into the picture as the illegitimate son of a murder suspect.

'Now, here's what I want you to do. You have been to the motel. You were to meet Dowling. You were to discuss matters pertaining to your son's welfare. You found Dowling dead, presumably murdered. You dashed out to a telephone booth so that you could notify the police, but before you could call, the police arrived. In some manner you felt they had found out about the murder.'

'But how was I to know that?'

'The police car passed you and turned in to the motel.'

'But I didn't see –'

'The police car passed you and turned in to the motel,' I said firmly.

She hesitated a moment, then said: 'Yes, Donald.'

'And,' I said, 'under the circumstances you think that your son is in danger. Where is he?'

'I have never disclosed the address to anyone.'

'That's fine,' I said. 'Keep that attitude and anyone

can find your son's address by paying the price of a morning paper.'

'He's at the Osgood Home. It's operated by Mrs Lillian Osgood. She took over after her husband's death.'

'Where is this home?'

'It's up in the mountains, about eleven miles from Banning.'

'What facilities for parents who want to visit the children?' I asked.

'There are motels in Banning. That's the closest place.'

'What is the name under which your son is registered?'

'Herbert Addis.'

'You gave him your name?'

'Yes.'

'You think your son is in danger,' I said. 'You are frantic. You go up to Banning to be near him. You start at once. His father has been killed. You think the father's murderer intends to kill the boy.'

'Why should he?' she asked.

'Dammit!' I told her. 'Don't argue with me! How do you know why Dowling was killed? There's every possibility that the person who killed Dowling was actuated by a fit of jealous rage and intends to kill your son. Even now the murderer may be speeding towards Banning to –'

'Donald, stop it! Do you hear me? Stop it! I'll –'

'You'll do exactly what I tell you,' I said. 'You're unnerved. You're almost hysterical. You're worrying about your son. It's only natural that you go to him. You get in your car and you go to Banning immediately. You register under your own name in a motel. You give the licence number of your car. You'll be very careful that you give the right licence number. You stay there where you can be near your son. In that way, if the police find out all about you and should play the right hunch, they can find you. But the chances that they will find you within the next twenty-four hours are rather slim – unless someone should tip them off. Even so, they won't think to look for you there at first.

'On the other hand, that won't be flight. It will be the natural reaction of a mother, the desire to be near her child and protect him from danger.

'If you have to explain that to a jury, there will be women on the jury and they will understand your position and your emotions. The police can't claim that you have resorted to flight. The women jurors will nod sympathetically and wipe away a tear.'

Irene Addis thought it over, then said: 'After what you've told me, Donald, I'd go to him no matter what the reason – You *may* be right. He may be in danger.'

I walked to the door, paused with my hand on the knob. 'Remember,' I said, 'that I told you your son was in danger.'

She came across the room with quick strides, put her hand over mine, holding it on the door-knob, stood close to me. 'Donald, why do you say that?'

'So you can remember that I said it.'

'And why should I remember that you said it?'

'It gives you all the reason you need, all the excuse you need, for hurrying to your son.'

She let the words soak in, then suddenly she was standing very close to me, her eyes looking steadfastly into mine. 'I can't tell you how I feel, Donald,' she said. 'There aren't those words in language.'

Then she drew away from me, smiled, and I opened the door and went out.

Chapter 9

I took a night plane to San Francisco, went to a hotel, registered under my own name, left a call for seven-thirty and went to sleep.

In the morning I shaved, had breakfast, and by nine o'clock was at the San Francisco office of the Electronic Investigative Equipment Company.

They had just opened up. I purchased an electronic shadowing device, complete with the part for the automobile of the investigator and the small broadcasting device which attached to the rear bumper of the car that was to be shadowed.

I hired a taxi to take me across to the Oakland Airport and, midway across the span of the Bay Bridge, tossed the receiving part of the electronic shadowing device through the cab window and down into the bay, retaining only the small part which clipped on to the bumper of the car that was to be shadowed.

At the Oakland Airport I roughed this part up a little bit, spattered it with some mud, put it in my brief-case and caught a Convair to Los Angeles.

I went to the parking lot, reclaimed the agency car, put the part of the shadowing device I had bought in San Francisco in the same package with the electronic device I retained from the job of shadowing Dowling, wrapped them all up together in a grimy cloth, and went up to the office.

It was one o'clock in the afternoon when Elsie put down the scissors and the newspapers and looked up as I opened the door.

'Donald!' she exclaimed.

'In person,' I told her.

'Donald, you didn't report. We don't know where you've been. You –'

'I was working on a case,' I said.

'Bertha's been trying to reach you all morning and right now she's positively screaming. Your client is in the office with her.'

'Carson?' I asked.

Elsie nodded, said: 'She wanted to be notified the very minute you came in the door.'

'All right,' I said, 'I'm in the door. Get her on the intercom and tell her – No, wait a minute, I'll go over myself and let her know I'm here.'

'I'd better give her a ring and tell her you're on your way,' she said.

'Okay, do that,' I said.

Elsie picked up the telephone, punched the button for Bertha's line, waited a moment, then said: 'Mr Lam just came in, Mrs Cool. I told him you wanted to see him . . .'

She held the instrument a couple of feet away from her ear so that her ear-drum wasn't hurt by the resulting blast of indignation from Bertha, then said: 'He's on his way in, Mrs Cool. . . . Yes, on his way.'

Elsie hung up.

I patted her shoulder, said: 'Don't let it get you down, kid,' and walked across to the door of Bertha's office.

Bertha Cool was sitting in the squeaky swivel chair at her desk, her lips tightly compressed with indignation, her eyes hard diamonds.

Montrose L. Carson sat in the client's chair, and the calm dignity of his presence was all that prevented Bertha Cool from exploding.

'Where the hell,' she began, 'have you . . .' She caught herself, took a deep breath and said: 'I've been looking for you all morning, Donald.'

'Been working on the case,' I said casually. 'How are you, Mr Carson?'

Carson nodded his greeting. Bertha, apparently surprised at my casual manner, said: 'Good heavens, Donald, haven't you heard?'

'Heard what?' I asked.

'About Dowling.'

'What about him?'

'He's been murdered.'

'What!'

'That's right. What's more, Sergeant Frank Sellers has been trying to get in touch with you. He's called up three times. He says he's to be notified the minute you get to the office – the very first minute.'

'Well,' I said, 'I guess we have about ten seconds to go then.'

Bertha glared at me, picked up the telephone and said to the office switchboard operator: 'Get me Sergeant Sellers.'

Bertha was still on the phone when the door was pushed open and Sergeant Sellers himself stood on the threshold making a somewhat dour appraisal of the situation.

'Thought I told you to call me . . .'

Bertha hung up the phone and said: 'I *was* calling you, dammit! You walked in right in the middle of the call.'

'That,' Sellers said, 'is what I call coincidence – a remarkable coincidence.'

Bertha said: 'Fry me for an oyster! I don't lie to you and you ought to know it. Go out and ask the operator what number I was calling. I don't lie to you, Frank Sellers. I don't have to.'

Sellers tilted the policeman's cap to the back of his head, shifted the half-chewed cigar from one corner of his mouth to the other. 'I want to talk with you folks,' he said.

'We have a client here,' Bertha told Sellers.

'Your client can go out and wait in the outer office,' Sellers said. 'The police don't wait.'

Carson said: 'I'm a taxpayer.'

Sellers looked at him thoughtfully. 'What's the name?'

'Montrose Levining Carson,' Carson said belligerently. 'Perhaps you'd like one of my cards.'

Sellers came over, extended a big hand, took the card, looked at it, pushed it into his pocket.

I said to Bertha: 'I'm quite sure Mr Carson wouldn't object to stepping out in the other office and –'

'Nonsense,' Bertha interrupted. 'He's a client. Frank Sellers, if you have anything to say, say it right here and then get out.'

Sellers shifted the cigar, looked at me thoughtfully, then back to Bertha, said: 'Okay, I'll say it right here. Herbert Jason Dowling was killed last night. He was murdered. Shot with a twenty-two-calibre automatic, in the *back* of the head. Would that mean anything to you folks?'

Carson started to say something. I said: 'We read the papers, Sellers.'

Sellers said: 'It isn't in the papers – not yet.'

I said with complete assurance: 'It's on the radio.'

'That isn't what you said.'

'It's what I meant.'

Sellers said: 'All right, I'll tell you something. Some private detective was working on Dowling at the time of his murder. We want to talk with that detective.'

I looked at Bertha. 'Dowling? Dowling?' I said, as though trying to recall the name.

Carson started to say something once more. I said: 'How do you know a private detective was working on him, Sergeant?'

'All right, I'll tell you how I know,' Sellers said. 'Because someone had his car bugged with an electronic shadowing device. Now, I've checked with the company that sells those devices here to find out the private detective agencies that have purchased those. They've sold about a dozen of them here in the city. You folks bought one. I have men chasing all the purchasers down. But with you, Pint Size, I decided to handle the interview personally.'

'Why?' I asked.

'Because,' he said, 'I'm naturally suspicious of you. You don't play square. You cut corners. . . . Now then, we won't have any argument. I want to know where your electronic shadowing device is, and I want to see both parts of it. You get me, Pint Size? *Both* parts!'

I said: 'It's in the agency car.'

'Where's the agency car?'

'Down at the lot.'

'Okay,' Sellers said, 'we'll go down to the lot and take a look. I just want to see that both parts are there. Now then, there's no use arguing, there's no use asking a lot of questions. The police are busy and it looks like you're busy. You just come right down to the agency car and show me *both* parts of the electronic shadowing device that you bought four months ago. If *both* parts are there, I'm going about my business and you can go about yours.'

I said wearily to Bertha: 'You'll have to excuse me, I guess.'

Bertha started to say something. I said to Sellers: 'That's all you want, Sergeant? Just to see the two parts?'

'That's all I want,' Sellers said, and then added almost as an afterthought, 'now.'

'Come on,' I told him, 'let's go.'

I turned to Carson and said: 'You'll excuse me, Mr Carson.'

He cleared his throat as though preparing to make a statement.

I turned and slid past Sellers and out of the door. 'Hey,' Sellers said, 'don't do that.'

'Don't do what?'

'You're supposed to be polite and hold the door open for me. Don't think you're going to slip down there and do any juggling with anything.'

'What would I juggle?' I asked.

'Damned if I know,' Sellers said. 'I don't trust you out of my sight.'

He strode out of Bertha Cool's private office and kicked the door shut behind him.

We went down in the elevator to the parking lot. I

opened the door of the car, said: 'We keep the thing in a special compartment under the seat.'

I pulled out the worn cloth, unwrapped it and showed him the two parts of the electronic shadowing device.

Sellers grunted, said: 'Okay, Pint Size, put it back. I was just checking, that's all.'

'Who's Dowling?' I asked.

'Some rich guy who had a date with a broad at a motel,' Sellers said, 'and somebody had his car bugged for a tailing job. I'd sure like to find out who it was.'

'Think you can do it?'

'Of course we can do it,' Sellers said. 'There have only been a limited number of those electronic shadowing devices sold in the city. Within a couple of hours we'll have every one of them run down. When I find the one that has the missing part, I'll find my man.'

'Then you don't want to question me about Dowling?'

He laughed and pulled the soggy cigar out of his mouth to use the moist end as a pointer to emphasize his gestures and words.

'No, Pint Size,' he said. 'I don't want to question you about it. You're a delightful little personality. You love to act dumb. You ask questions. When you ask questions, you're getting answers. When you're getting answers, you get information. When you get information, you try to turn it to account. You want to make a profit on everything that you can get hold of. If I told you everything I know, then you'd know as much as I do, and that might be too damn much. If I start asking you questions, you'll start asking me questions, and the first thing I know I'll be giving you information you don't have and can't get. Just go on back to your office now. Be a good boy and keep your nose clean. Otherwise Papa's going to spank, and if Papa spanks, it's going to hurt you a hell of a lot worse than it does me.'

Sellers turned and strode off.

I went back to the office.

Carson looked at me respectfully and said: 'I tried twice to tell the officer that you were interested in Dowling.'

I looked at Carson with blank amazement. 'That *I* was interested in Dowling?' I asked.

'Why, certainly.'

'I don't know what gave you any reason to think that,' I said.

'Well, weren't you?'

I said: 'Look here, Mr Carson. Let's not get things mixed up. You hired us to find out about a leak in your organization. I believe *you* felt that Dowling was the recipient of information that was being stolen from you, but *we* certainly weren't retained to investigate Dowling. Did you think we were?'

'Well . . .' He hesitated.

'If you were going to investigate Dowling,' I said, 'it would have necessarily been upon an entirely different financial arrangement.'

'I thought we should have told the officer,' Carson finished lamely.

Bertha said: 'Dammit to hell, Donald, what are you trying to pull? You should have told Frank Sellers what the facts were.'

'Well, what *were* the facts?' I asked innocently.

'You know.'

'Certainly I know,' I said. 'Now let *me* tell *you* something. Both you folks were all primed to spill information to Sellers. It was information he had no right to receive. An officer is never entitled to know the identity of a client unless that identity plays a significant part in a case the officer is investigating.

'In your case, Carson, you're the head of a corporation. You have a duty to stockholders. The minute you told Sellers that you had retained us to investigate Dowling, he would have put an entirely wrong interpretation upon your statement. What's more to the point, he would have given it to the press. An officer in Sellers's position can't hold out on the newspapers even if he wants to, and he doesn't try very hard.

'How would you like it if your stockholders read in the papers that you had retained a firm of private detectives to investigate a competitor and that a detective was shadowing that competitor when he was murdered?'

'Good God!' Carson said, his facial expression altering from one of dignity to one of almost ludicrous dismay.

'Now you get the sketch,' I told him. 'I kept both of you from blabbing something that Sellers had no right to know.'

'I don't blab,' Bertha said indignantly. 'I resent your intimating that I do.'

Carson was thoughtful for a moment, then he got up from his chair, came stalking over and took my hand in his big, bony paw and pumped my arm up and down.

'Lam,' he said, 'I owe you a debt of gratitude!'

'And now,' I told him, 'since Dowling is dead, there is no longer any reason for you to have us investigating the leak in your business. Therefore, if anyone should ask you if you are employing the firm of Cool and Lam, you can truthfully tell them that you are not. Then you can think awhile and say that they *have* done work for you in the past and you might very well retain them in the future if anything should come up, but they are not representing you in any way at the present time.'

Bertha Cool said angrily: 'What the hell are you trying to do, get us fired?'

Carson turned to her and said: 'You are not fired, Mrs Cool. You have, so to speak, worked yourself out of a job. I was about to point that out to you. It was the main reason for my visit this morning.'

'Now look,' Bertha said, 'don't think anybody can hold out on Frank Sellers. Now, what happened when he found out the part of our electronic shadowing device was missing?'

'Was it missing?' I asked.

'Dammit!' Bertha shouted at me. 'Come down to earth. Quit dodging around. What did he say?'

'He told me to go back up to the office and mind my own business. He told me that he didn't want to ask me any questions about Dowling and he didn't want me to ask him any questions. He said that whenever I got to talking with him I had a way of prying information out of him and always got better than I gave and to hell with us.'

Bertha looked at me in open-mouthed amazement. 'You mean that the part was there?' she asked.

'If it hadn't been, do you think I'd have been here or at police headquarters?'

'Fry me for an oyster!' Bertha said.

Carson had been thinking things over. 'I am sure Mr Lam is right, Mrs Cool,' he said, with painstaking deliberation.

'You don't know Frank Sellers,' Bertha Cool said grimly.

Carson placed the tips of his fingers together, gave Bertha Cool a bushy-browed steady stare and said: 'Nor does Frank Sellers know me.'

I stretched, yawned, started for the door, said: 'Well, if you folks will pardon me, I've got fish to fry.'

Bertha Cool said: 'Now, you look here. I'm going to ring up Frank Sellers and tell him in confidence that . . . that . . .'

'Go ahead,' I said, watching the expression of gradually growing cold anger on Carson's face.

Bertha said: 'I'm going to tell him that we had a client who was interested in some of the things Dowling was doing.'

'I would suggest, Mrs Cool, that you do nothing of the sort,' Carson said.

'Now look,' Bertha pleaded, 'we can't do business if the police are down on us. We can't even keep our licence unless we keep our noses clean. Frank Sellers is working on a murder case. He knows that some detective agency was interested in Dowling and –'

'How does he know that?' Carson interrupted.

'Because of that electric bug.'

'Then let him find the agency which has the component part he is looking for,' Carson said.

'Fair enough,' I said, nodding.

Bertha's lips were tightly compressed. 'Nuts to both of you.'

Carson said: 'I beg your pardon, Mrs Cool. I am not accustomed to associating with women who use that sort of language.'

Bertha was good and mad now. 'You came to us and wanted information,' she said. 'We got it for you. Now leave me and my language out of it and don't tell me how to run my business. I'm going to ring up Frank Sellers and tell him the whole set-up.'

'That will be violating a professional confidence,' Carson said.

'This is a murder case, and Frank Sellers can play rough,' Bertha said.

Carson turned to her, his pin-point eyes hard and cold. 'If you violate a professional confidence and tell the police anything about this, I shall charge you with unprofessional conduct.'

He bowed and stalked from the office with all the synthetic dignity of a corporation president leaving a board meeting.

'Sonofabitch!' Bertha said.

'Me?' I asked.

'Him,' she said. And then after a moment of thoughtful silence, added: 'You, too. I have the feeling that you manipulated Carson's thinking so you could get yourself off a hot spot. I don't know what kind of a flim-flam you worked on Frank Sellers, showing him that gadget, but I'm willing to bet it was our bug on the back of Dowling's car. Now, get the hell out of here.'

I left her, walked down to my office and said to Elsie Brand: 'Elsie, you're going to have to cover for me.'

'How come?' she asked.

I said: 'You've got to remember that I had an important telephone call that came in – a seductive voice, a young woman's voice, who said that she had some important information for me about the case we were working on, and I was to meet her at the same place I'd seen her last night.'

Elsie shook her head and said: 'It won't work, Donald.'

'Why not?'

'They'd ask the switchboard operator about the voice and –'

'The switchboard operator wouldn't know anything,' I said. 'The woman would simply ask to be connected with my office. You'd talk with her and she would tell you what she wanted to see me about so then I'd get on the line.'

Elsie shook her head and said: 'There'd be no record of an incoming call.'

'Yes, there will be,' I said.

'How come?'

I said: 'You're going down the hall. While you're down there you'll place a call and ask for me. The operator will remember the call coming in. She won't remember that you weren't in the office, particularly if you go out the side door.'

'She'll know my voice.'

'Not if you disguise it and talk very rapidly. Appear to be tremendously excited.'

'She'll remember how long the phone was tied up on the connection,' Elsie said.

'Hang it,' I told her, 'get started. Don't worry about all the little things. Leave them to me. I'll talk long enough to keep the line busy for the proper interval.'

Elsie hesitated a moment, then slipped out of the side door and went down the hall.

A few moments later the phone rang.

I picked it up, said: 'Hello,' and heard Elsie's voice saying: 'Mr Lam, I've got a red-hot tip for you. I want you to meet me at once down at the place where I saw you last night.'

'How hot is the tip?'

'Red-hot.'

'Wonderful,' I said. 'Have you heard any good stories lately?'

'Donald, don't,' she said. 'The operator may cut in at any moment.'

'Then we'll fire her for listening.'

'No, I don't hear any *good* stories around that office.'

'Okay,' I said, 'we've been talking long enough. You can hang up now and come back to the office. Remember, if anyone asks for me, I went tearing out on a hot tip.'

'Donald, are you getting in trouble again?'

'Hell, no,' I told her. 'I'm getting out of trouble – at least I'm trying to.'

I hung up the phone, grabbed my hat and went tearing out of the office.

Chapter 10

I knew that within a couple of hours I was going to be hotter than a firecracker. The police would be looking for me, probably with an all-points bulletin.

I disguised my voice as best I could, called up the office and asked for Mr Lam.

The switchboard operator said: 'I'll connect you with his secretary.'

A moment later Elsie was on the line.

'Hi, Elsie,' I said, in my normal voice.

'Donald!' she gasped. 'Bertha's fit to be tied. Frank Sellers was here at the office and I guess there's . . . well, there's a *lot* of trouble.'

'There'll be more,' I told her. 'Now look, Elsie, that clipping that you were putting in the scrapbook about the Peeping Tom in the motel. As I remember it, that was several days old.'

'I just can't keep up with the crime situation, Donald,' she said. 'I –'

'Never mind that,' I said. 'Grab that scrapbook and give me the dope on it. I want the name of the woman.'

'All right,' she said. 'I'll get it for you.'

'Don't let anyone see what you're doing,' I said. 'If Bertha comes in the office or if Frank Sellers should come in, just hang up the phone, grab more clippings and start pasting them in the book.'

'Okay, just a minute, hold the phone, Donald.'

I held the phone for some fifteen seconds, then she said: 'Here it is, Donald. The woman was Agnes Dayton, twenty-six, living at three-six-seven Corinthian Arms Apartment in Santa Ana and registered there in the motel for the night.'

'Okay,' I said, 'I'll take it from there.'

'Donald, please be careful.'

'It's too late to be careful now,' I said. 'I'm in over my head, and the only thing to do is to start swimming.'

I hung up, rented a car, drove to Santa Ana and hunted up the Corinthian Arms Apartment. Sure enough, Apartment 367 was listed under the name of Agnes Dayton.

I pressed the mother-of-pearl button by the door and chimes sounded.

A moment later the door opened. A well-modulated voice said: 'Yes?' and then suddenly stopped with a gasping intake of breath.

The young woman who was looking at me with startled eyes was Bernice Clinton.

'Donald!' she said. 'How in the world did you ever find me here?'

'Why?' I asked. 'Weren't you supposed to be here?'

'This is . . . this is – Well, this isn't my regular . . .'
She stopped, confused.

'I know,' I said. 'This is a hide-out.'

'Donald, what . . . what do you want?'

'Right at present I want to come in and talk for a while.'

She hesitated, then opened the door. 'All right, she said, 'come in.'

The apartment had class stamped all over it. There was a well-furnished living-room, a swinging door leading to a kitchen, another door which I assumed led to a bedroom and there was a private balcony with picture windows opening off the living-room.

I said: 'I've been thinking over that proposition you made about the lease.'

She indicated a chair, turned her back to me for a moment, then turned around. I could see that she had been biting her lip. Her eyes had panic in them.

'Donald, how – I suppose you followed me, but I would have sworn you couldn't have followed me. I took *every* precaution.'

'Why?' I asked.

'I – All right, what do you want?'

'I just wanted to let you know that I'd decided to accept your offer on the lease.'

'I'm sorry, Donald, I'm truly sorry.'

'What's the matter?'

'The offer has been withdrawn. My principal –'

'Are you in the real estate business?'

'No, not exactly.'

'May I ask exactly what your occupation is?'

'Donald, please. . . . Please quit torturing me and tell me what it is you want.'

I put an expression of surprise on my face. 'What do I want? Why, I want to talk about the lease, of course.'

She gave that statement the scrutiny of a frowning concentration for a moment, then said: 'Look, Donald, I'm awfully sorry about this thing, about this whole business. I had a person who was stringing me along. He was talking about a fancy price for a lease on a corner lot, and now I'm satisfied the whole thing was phony. I'm awfully sorry if I gave you a false impression. I – Look, Donald, I'll do anything I can to make it up to you. I'm just terribly sorry, that's all.'

She was talking rapidly, the way a person does who wants to lie out of a situation and is trying to keep words going.

'That's all right, Bernice,' I said. 'Why give me an assumed name?'

'It's because . . . because – Oh, Donald, you've got me all mixed up and confused. I – All right, Donald, I'll come clean. I was sent to you for the purpose of getting that lease and I didn't want to give you this name and address. My real name *is* Bernice. The man who wanted the lease on your property was – Well, he's backed out now.'

'You won't take it at any price?'

'I'm sorry, Donald. I *can't* take it at any price. Look,' she said, 'I – Donald, be a good boy and forget about the whole thing, will you?'

She came over close to me, stood looking at me with thoughtful, contemplative eyes. 'Donald, please be a dear and skip the whole thing. . . . Come on, Donald, you can't stay here. I . . . I'm going out.'

I looked at the lounging pyjamas and raised my eyebrows.

'I'm going to dress. I've got an appointment at the beauty-shop and I've got to dress.'

I said: 'Why can't you make any offer on the lot now, Bernice?'

She said: 'Can't you understand, Donald? The man I was representing – he's backed out. He doesn't want it at any price. He's got something else.'

'You were representing a man?'

115

'Of course. *I* don't have that kind of money, Donald.'

I waved my hand around the apartment and said: 'You're not exactly suffering.'

She started to say something, then checked herself.

'Donald, please.' She came and gave me her hands, pulled me to my feet, looked me in the eyes for a moment, then suddenly melted into my arms and said: 'Donald, you're a dear! You . . . you *do* understand, don't you?'

'I guess so,' I said. 'I –'

'Donald, you're wonderful, you're sweet. Later on I'm going to show you how very, very much I appreciate what you're doing, but you'll have to go now.'

She was guiding me to the door. She held it open. 'Perhaps we can see each other some time again, Donald, on . . . well, you know . . . a proposition that I *won't* have to back out on.'

'On the corner lot?' I asked.

'On anything,' she said, gently pushing me into the corridor. She closed the door fast. I heard a bolt shoot into place.

I stood there listening. Faintly I could hear the sounds of hurried motion. Then I heard the whirring of a telephone dial.

I waited outside the door, listening, hoping I could hear the sound of her voice.

Apparently the number she was calling didn't answer because after a while she hung up and dialled again.

There was still no answer.

I went down the corridor to the elevator, got in my rented car and drove back to the city.

Chapter 11

Colley Norfolk had a theatrical booking agency that specialized in just about everything anybody could want. If you wanted talent for a stag party, Colley could find it. If you wanted a stripper for a hole-in-the-wall night spot, Colley was your man. Of course, his material wasn't A Number One top drawer, but they didn't get the highest prices.

I'd known Colley for a while and he knew me, but not too well. I caught him in his office, a little hole-in-the-wall place where he had a desk with four telephones. I knew that three of them were dummies. Only one was connected, but by pressing a foot on different buttons he could make any one of them ring.

The walls were plastered with autographed photographs of girls, big-busted babes, pin-up photographs, nudes and near nudes.

'What's cooking, Donald?' he said.

I said: 'I want a stripper who's hungry.'

'Hell, they're all hungry.'

'I want one that's hungry and wants work. I want one that could use a little high-class publicity and when she got it, it wouldn't be wasted.'

'What do you mean by that?'

'I don't want someone who's old enough to sag. I

want someone who's young enough to have a reasonable figure and a good personality. I want one who's at the beginning of her career instead of at the end.'

'What do you want her for?'

'I want to give her some publicity.'

'In return for what?'

'In return for service.'

Colley straightened up at the desk.

One of the dummy phones rang.

Colley said: 'Excuse me a minute,' picked up the receiver and said: 'Hello. . . . Yeah, this is Colley. . . . Oh, you're ready to close, huh? . . . At five hundred a week. . . . To hell with that stuff. I told you I wouldn't take less than seven fifty. . . . Well, this babe isn't in the five-hundred-dollar-a-week class and I don't propose to get her there. I . . .'

Abruptly he looked at me and said: 'Oh, hell. I forgot you were wise to this crap,' and slammed the dummy receiver back on the hook. Then he grinned and said: 'You want me to make the approach to this babe, or do you?'

'I do.'

Colley thumbed through a card index and said: 'Look. Here's a kid who's been on the turf. She knows her way around, but she's young.'

'How young?'

'Twenty-two.'

'Come again,' I said.

He grinned. 'All right, maybe twenty-six, but she can pass for twenty-two, and she's doing it.'

'What experience?'

'Well, it depends on what you mean by experience,' he said. 'She's done stripping at little joints and thought she was good. She came to the big time and thought it would be easy.'

'Got anything on the ball?'

'I think she has. I've never seen her strip, but she's built. I think she might go if she could get her start.'

'What's her name?'

'Daffidill Lawson.'

'Come again.'

'That's the only name I have,' he said. 'Here, I'll give you her address. You go talk with her. Remember, if anything comes of it I want my cut.'

'You get your ten per cent on what booking she gets, provided you've got her tied up under a contract.'

'I've got her tied up,' he said, 'but she doesn't want to stay tied up. She's getting restless. She thinks that I should get her placed somewhere. She thinks I should be doing something. She rings me up a couple of times a day – dammit, I guess she's really hungry.'

'Give me her address.'

He copied the address from the card and shoved the scrawled paper across the desk.

'Remember,' he said, '*I* contacted *you* and dreamed this thing up. It isn't *your* idea.'

'Do I look dumb?' I asked. 'I wouldn't let you down when you're co-operating.'

'Hell, I should have known,' he said, 'but the woods hereabouts are full of chisellers. Go to it, and lots of luck. Tell her to call me if she's in doubt about anything.'

'I'll give it a whirl,' I said.

I didn't dare use the agency car any more. They might have an all-points bulletin out for it. It was a cinch that after Bertha called, Frank Sellers would be smart enough to think of the San Francisco angle and would have called up the Electronics Investigative Equipment branch up there. By the time he'd talked with them he'd be gunning for me with heavy-calibre bullets.

I took a cab out to the address Colley had given me. It was a shoddy place that had a big sign APARTMENTS out in front, but was really a second-rate rooming house that was pretty run down at the heels.

I climbed the stairs and walked down to Daffidill Lawson's apartment. I knocked on the door.

A feminine voice called: 'Who is it?'

'I'm representing Colley Norfolk,' I said. 'I want to talk with you.'

The door opened a crack. Dark, intense eyes surveyed me thoughtfully, then the door opened all the way. 'What's your name?' she asked.

'Donald,' I said.

'What's your other name?'

'I haven't any.'

'That's not a good approach,' she said.

'By the time you get older,' I told her, 'you'll know it isn't the approach that counts, it's the finish. Lots of people have a good approach.'

There was one chair in the room. She indicated I should take it. She sat on the edge of the bed, with its pancake-thin mattress, and crossed her legs.

'What do you want?'

'I'm publicity,' I said. 'Colley told me you needed some publicity.'

'So he finally woke up, did he?' she asked.

'Hell,' I said, 'he's been awake all the time, but this is a tough racket.'

'Are you telling me? What's the dodge?'

I said: 'This is going to be good, but you have to be good to take advantage of it. You have to be a good little actress to put it across.'

'What do I put across?'

I said: 'Have you seen the papers today?'

'Don't be silly,' she said. 'Papers cost money. I haven't seen breakfast yet. And if that lousy agent doesn't kick up with something pretty soon, I won't even see my one two-bit meal a day.'

I said: 'He's kicked up with me.'

'Well, what good are you?'

'For one thing,' I said, 'I represent food. Can you get anything sent up here?'

'How would I know?' she asked. 'There's a hamburger joint down at the corner.'

'Any restaurant with booths?'

'Say, you're talking big. You must have a *real* idea.'

'I have.'

'Boy, I could sure use coffee and thick hamburgers,' she said.

'How about a good thick steak with French fried potatoes?'

'Are you kidding?'

'Try me out.'

She was on her feet instantly, looked down at her legs, walked to a drawer, pulled out a pair of nylons and sat on the bed while she put them on, then pulled her skirt up, straightened the stockings, looked at her legs approvingly and said: 'I have to take care of my few remaining stockings. Those legs are what's going to get me by.'

'They're good,' I said.

121

'Like them?'

'I sure do. They've got what it takes.'

'Take a good look,' she invited.

The skirt went up.

I took a good look.

'What do you think?'

'I think they're absolutely first-class. They should get you by in the big time.'

'Lots of people tell me that, but . . . well, here I am. Broke and hungry.'

'But in a big city.'

'In a big city.'

'And you're about to eat,' I told her.

We went down to the street, passed up the hamburger joint which really smelled good, and went to the restaurant with booths. She had a steak, French fried potatoes and coffee. I couldn't get her to take any dessert.

'I'm watching my figure,' she said. 'I have to.'

'I am, too,' I told her.

'You haven't seen it yet.'

'It looks all right from what I've seen.'

'It's all all right,' she told me. 'It will get me by if I can only get the opportunity to show it.'

'Okay,' I said, 'let's go back to your place. I want to tell you about it.'

She finished the last of the coffee, gave a sigh of deep contentment and we walked back.

'All right,' she said. 'What do I do?'

'You strip,' I told her.

'That's fine. I'm good at it,' she said, walking around the room humming a little tune, swaying her hips, her hands fumbling at a zipper, her eyes provocative.

'But,' I said, 'you do it in a peculiar way.'

'How come?' she asked, her hips continuing to sway slightly.

I said: 'If you had been reading the papers, you would know that there's a motel down at the beach, The Swim and Tan Motel. They've been having trouble with a Peeping Tom.'

'Those bastards,' she said. 'My God, Donald, why is it that men want to look surreptitiously when it wouldn't do them any possible good? What do they think, a girl undressing in a bedroom and seeing some stranger standing outside is going to smile at him and say: "Oh, hello. I didn't know you were watching. Wouldn't you like to come in?"'

I said: 'Men like to watch women undress. That's what makes you a living.'

'A hell of a living,' she said.

'It's going to get better from now on.'

'What's the gag?'

'Just this,' I said. 'There have been several complaints of a Peeping Tom at the Swim and Tan Motel. The police haven't done too much about it. They go down there with a prowl car and look the place over, and when a patrol car goes by they're under orders to keep an eye open just to see if there's anybody walking around that can't give a good account of himself.'

'Go on,' she said.

'Then last night,' I told her, 'there was a murder in the place.'

'A murder?'

I nodded.

'Nix,' she said.

'What do you mean, nix?'

'I mean no, nothing doing. Take it away. Thanks for the steak and potatoes. You're a nice guy. I enjoyed meeting you. Get another idea sometime when you have money enough for a meal and come on up. On second thought, if you don't have any ideas but have money enough for a meal, come on up, any way.'

'Don't guys that have money enough for meals always have ideas?' I asked.

She grinned and said: 'Guys that have ideas don't always have money enough for meals.'

'Calm down,' I told her, 'take it easy, and listen. The murder has naturally got the police on edge.'

'It's got me on edge.'

I said: 'The police are going to be looking for the Peeping Tom.'

'That's natural.'

'They won't know where to look.'

'So what do I do? Show them where he is?'

'You show them where he is.'

'How nice. How do I know where he is?'

I said: 'You're bait. You're window dressing.'

She started to say something, then caught herself. 'Window dressing?'

I nodded. 'Window undressing.'

She thought things over for a moment, then slowly a smile began to lift the corners of her mouth. 'Go on, Donald. Tell me more.'

'That's all there is to it,' I said. 'You check into a motel this afternoon. You forget to pull the shade on the back window. That's one reason that motel has been having trouble. Most motels have the windows in the front and at the back there's nothing except a small bathroom window that is covered with ground glass. These units have a window in back.

'You get in the place and start stripping. You aren't in a hurry. You take off a little something and then putter around doing things to your hair and one thing and another, then you take off more.'

'What happens after I've got it all off? Then the police would arrest me for indecent exposure.'

'What are you talking about?' I said. 'You're in a private room. You've just forgot to pull the curtain. The police have no business looking.'

She let the idea soak in.

'Suppose I draw a blank?' she said. 'I can't stay there all night taking things off, particularly after I've got them all off.'

'After you've taken off as much as you care to,' I said, 'you –'

'As much as I dare to,' she interrupted.

'All right, have it either way,' I said. 'After you've taken off as much as you dare to, you go into the shower. You take a shower, come out and put on clothes. You dress very quickly. Then you wait a few minutes and start taking them off again. You keep doing your routine until we get a customer.'

'How do we know when we get a customer?' she asked.

I said: 'There's a hotel about half a block away. I'm going to get a room on the side that faces the back of the Swim and Tan Motel. I'm going to be watching your unit through binoculars. If anybody shows up and starts watching, I can see him. If and when he does, I'll turn on a red light in my room and leave the window up. From time to time as you walk past your window in the motel you can just glance casually out of the corner of your eye. If you see a red light, you'll know the man is there.'

'Then what?'

'Then,' I said, 'you telephone the police that there's a Peeping Tom.'

'And he becomes alarmed and takes off?'

'That,' I said, 'is the difference between an amateur stripper and a professional stripper. When the amateur discovers a man, she screams and rushes for the telephone. She starts covering up. You don't scream, you don't dash for the telephone, you don't cover anything. You move over slowly. The telephone is out of range of the window. You do it in such a way that the Peeping Tom wants more – and sticks around. After you finish stripping and go into the wings, the audience doesn't get up and walk out, does it?'

She shook her head.

'What does it do?'

'If I've got them properly warmed up, they applaud to beat hell,' she said. 'They want me to come back and go all the way.'

I said: 'If you do a good professional job, the Peeping Tom will be there.'

'Then what?'

'Then the police come and catch him.'

'Then what?'

'Then they knock on your door and say: 'Lady, you shouldn't undress with the curtains up. Don't you know better than that?'

'And then what do I say?'

'Then,' I said, 'you tell them that you were just helping the police trap a murderer, that was all. That your friend, Colley Norfolk, thought that it would be good publicity. He thought that if you could hold a murderer spellbound until the police arrived, it would be a service for suffering humanity and swell publicity for you.

'About that time Colley Norfolk picks up the telephone and calls the newspapers and says: 'Boys, here's a new angle. Professional stripper has Peeping Tom arrested.'

She thought that over for several seconds and then the smile that had been at the corners of her mouth became a grin.

'Like it?' I asked.

'I *love* it!' she said.

I got up and started for the door.

'Want to rehearse me any?' she asked.

'No, I'm satisfied you can do it all right.'

'Want to see my technique?'

'I'll be looking at your technique tonight,' I said, 'through binoculars. Here's twenty bucks expense money.'

I put twenty dollars on the shaky little bedroom night stand and headed for the door.

She grinned and blew me a kiss.

I went out, rented a car, and drove to the hotel on the beach.

It was easy to see the trouble with the hotel. It had a nice location, but the rooms were about two hundred per cent over-priced.

I looked the place over. There were lots of vacant rooms. The clerk wanted to give me a room on the ocean front. I told him I couldn't afford the price and would take one in back. I looked over several rooms.

I finally got the room I wanted.

I picked up the telephone, called the rooming house where Daffidill Lawson was staying, and told her to get ready to take a ride.

I went back to the city in my drive-yourself car, picked her up and took her to the Swim and Tan Motel. I had on heavy dark glasses and had piled the car with suitcases.

'Number nine is the best one for our purpose,' I said. 'You look at all of them, Be a little particular. Finally settle on number nine because the air in it is better.'

Daffidill did a good job. The manager was a little annoyed by the time the stripper had looked through three other places before settling on 9.

Unit 12 was closed up with the curtains drawn. Evidently the police were finished with it, but there probably were still sinister red stains on the floor and the motel manager wasn't renting it.

'Your husband sign the register?' the manager asked.

Daffidill grinned and said: 'I do all the secretarial work in the family. He pays the bills.'

She extended a hand and wiggled her fingers.

I put bills in it.

We took the key, went up to the place and I lifted out suitcases. They were for the most part filled with old telephone directories, but they looked impressive.

Daffidill walked over to the back window, took a good look at it, and said: 'No wonder they have Peeping Toms.'

I nodded.

'What do we do now?' she asked. She started walking, humming a tune, swaying her hips. Her hand went slowly back to the zipper.

'Feel like you could eat again?' I asked.

'My stomach does but my figure doesn't.'

'We've got to stick around a while,' I said. 'We don't want the manager to get suspicious.'

'What do you mean, stick around?'

'We're going to have to stay here for a while.'

'All right,' she said, 'I'll put it up to you cold turkey. When do you make passes?'

'I don't make any.'

'Why?'

'Because I've got to do a lot of thinking.'

She said: 'My stomach's purring with contentment. I want to doze off for a siesta. Are you on the up and up?'

'I'm on the up and up,' I told her.

She pulled the zipper, eased out of her dress. She did it with seductive skill, making her hand motion seem to caress the curves of her body as she wriggled out of it.

'Hey,' I said, 'that promise was provisional. Don't make it look so tempting.'

'You haven't seen anything yet,' she said. 'Wait until tonight.'

She draped the dress over a hanger, kicked her shoes off, slowly removed her stockings, went to the bed and lay down.

'Cover me up, Donald.'

I put the blanket over her.

After a few moments she was sound asleep, a natural kid sleep that softened her features and made her look five years younger. She really had curves and they were in the right places.

After a while I kicked my coat and shoes off and stretched out in the chair. It was uncomfortable. To hell with it. I went over and got on the other side of the bed.

After a while I went to sleep. I'd been covering a lot of ground and was tired.

It was quite dark when I awakened. She was lying on one elbow looking down at me and there was enough light coming in from the electric sign that flickered on and off so I could see her smiling.

'Know something, Donald?'

'What?'

'You're too damn good to be true.'

Then she kissed me.

She straightened and ran her fingers through my hair. 'If this works,' she said. 'Oh, gosh, Donald, how I hope it works!'

'It'll work,' I told her.

She kissed me again.

Chapter 12

After a while I left the motel, went over to the hotel room, turned out the lights, pulled up a chair so that I was seated comfortably, adjusted binoculars, placed a spotlight with a red lens on it on the table at my right hand, and focused the binoculars on the lighted window of Unit 9.

It was about fifteen minutes before Daffidill Lawson followed instructions and went to work.

The girl was good.

She took off her garments, and it took her about fifteen minutes for each garment. She was standing in front of a mirror, looking at herself with an expression of voluptuous admiration, as though she felt those feminine curves constituted the reason she had been created in the first place.

After the outer garments, she took off the stockings, one at a time, putting her leg up on a chair, rolling the stockings down carefully, smoothly, and then walking around.

By this time it was apparent she was a woman undressing and was intending to go all the way. Anybody who had been watching would have been completely hypnotized.

Despite the fact that I knew it was a professional job

and that she was posing, my eyes were pushing at the binoculars. Once she turned to the back window and blew a kiss. I knew she knew I was watching and that the kiss was for me. Despite that knowledge I became irritated. It was a break in the professional art. It wasn't in character. She was supposed to be a woman undressing in a motel unit.

I thought of phoning her to cut it out. She was supposed to be baiting a trap, not flirting with me.

Also it was apparent that pretty soon she was going to have to begin all over again. She'd completed the first act.

It was then I saw him, a furtive head silhouetted for a moment against the window, then back out of sight. Then a shadowy figure moving around the back of the motel. Then the head framed against the light again.

I waited until Daffidill had her face pointed towards the window and flashed on the red spotlight, kept it on for three or four seconds, then switched it off.

She moved easily and naturally, stepping out of the picture for just long enough to call the police. Then she was back in front of the mirror.

Heaven knows how she prolonged the suspense the way she did. Watching her through the binoculars, I almost forgot about the Peeping Tom, I was so interested in watching.

The man who had been looking in the window was all eyes now. He was standing perfectly still, his head and shoulders silhouetted against the lighted window.

Daffidill Lawson stood in front of the mirror and looked at herself, taking what might be called a physical inventory.

Then abruptly there was the flurry of motion. Two men became silhouetted in the lighted oblong. The

Peeping Tom heard them, turned, gave one startled gasp and started to run.

Daffidill Lawson jumped to her feet.

Then she walked over to the window, blew another kiss in the direction of the hotel window where I was watching, and pulled the shade.

That was it. I had sprung a trap and it had caught something. I could read what it was in the papers the next day – provided I could keep out of jail that long myself.

I sat there in the dark, thinking things over. Bernice Clinton, with an apartment in the Corinthian Arms in Santa Ana, as Agnes Dayton; the mysterious Peeping Tom at the motel; the murder of Herbert Dowling; Irene Addis with her young son in the boys' home above Banning.

I wondered if I should get in touch with her and see if she was all right.

Then abruptly there was a knock at the door.

I stiffened. Apparently my cover-up hadn't been good enough. Well, there was no use trying to stall it off.

I walked to the door and flung it open, ready to have Frank Sellers grab me by the neck-tie, jerk me out into the hall, slam me up against the wall and ask me who the hell I thought I was kidding.

Daffidill Lawson stood there on the threshold with a smile on her face.

'How did I do?' she asked.

Chapter 13

'Well, we did it. It worked,' Daffidill said. 'Tell me, Donald, will I get the publicity?'

'You'll get the publicity,' I told her, 'but I want to know just what happened.'

'What happened?' she exclaimed, her voice showing her disappointment. 'Weren't you watching, for Pete's sake? It was one of the best strips I ever did!'

'I saw the strip,' I told her. 'I want to know what happened after that.'

She stood close to me. Her right hand crept up around my neck; the fingers played with my hair. Her eyes had that look of exultant triumph which transcends passion; the look which comes to the eyes of a hungry actress who is assured of front-page publicity.

'Oh, Donald!' she said ecstatically, and kissed me.

It was quite some kiss.

'Donald,' she said, as I closed the door, 'you're a genius. You're . . .'

'Colley Norfolk is the one who thought up the publicity angle,' I said.

'Baloney,' she told me. 'Colley never had that much brains in his whole head. I'll ride along with the gag if you want, but I know who thought it up. Tell me, Donald, how did I do?'

She crossed the darkened room to stand at the window, looking over towards the motel. Then she picked up the binoculars which were on the table and looked at the lighted room.

'I'll bet you could see me just as plain as plain,' she said, and laughed; a little throaty seductive laugh. 'How did I do, Donald?'

'You were wonderful,' I said.

'That's professional stuff you saw, Donald. Any woman can take her clothes off; but to strip so that people go absolutely crazy with suspense – well, that takes a little doing.'

'You did it.'

'Did you get a thrill, Donald?'

'And how!'

'I'll bet with these binoculars you felt that you could reach out and put your hand on me.'

'Not through a pane of glass here and a screen and a window in the motel,' I said.

She laughed again. 'Well, there's no glass here now,' she said.

I said: 'If we're going to make the morning papers, you'll have to tell me what happened. Then I've got to get Colley on the phone and he can get the reporters.'

'Then what do they do?' she asked.

'Stick around and listen to the telephone conversation,' I said.

'Don't think I'm not going to.'

'Did the police ask you questions?'

'Very, very few. They were so interested in getting this Peeping Tom that they didn't bother about anything else. They certainly *really* wanted him.'

'Who was he?'

'Some peculiar character by the name of Rossiter Banks.'

'Any middle initial?' I asked.

'D, for Dudley,' she said. 'He had his driving licence. Believe me, the police took him to pieces. They brought him into the room after I'd put my clothes on, and asked me to identify him.'

'Did you identify him?'

'Sure.'

'Was he the man?'

'Of course.'

'You saw his face?'

'I saw his face,' she said, 'and he saw a lot more of me than that.' She laughed. 'Boy, you should have seen his eyes bulging out. He was standing there at the window and so completely, utterly fascinated he never thought about the light streaming out on his face. His mouth was open – it looked like a foot wide. Boy, was he getting an eyeful and was he completely hypnotized by what he saw!'

'Banks,' I said. 'Did you find out anything about him?'

'I found out *all* about him. The police questioned him for a while before they took him away and he was blurting out his story – it was all on account of you, Donald.'

'What do you mean, all on account of me? I told you it was Colley who –'

'I didn't mean that, Donald. I mean he was hanging around the place because of you.'

'Oh?' I asked.

'Uh-huh. He's the manager of a branch telegraph office. It's not a big office but it seems that it's strategically located because it's in the district where a police officer by the name of Sellers lives.'

I sat own abruptly. I could feel a preliminary chill rippling up my backbone. The warmth engendered by her kiss vanished as though someone had given me a blood transfusion of ice water. My pounding pulse dropped back to normal. 'What about it?' I asked.

'Well, it seems that this police officer, Sellers, wired to some electronic outfit in San Francisco, giving a description of you and your name and asking if, by any chance, you had purchased an electronic shadowing device for automobiles within the last forty-eight hours. He got back an answer that you had.'

'What did Banks say about me?' I asked.

'Well, Banks said that you were making a play for one of the women employees in the office and that he thought that perhaps you'd made a date down here at the Swim and Tan Motel because Sellers had sent a wire to someone stating that a Robert C. Richards, who had registered at the Swim and Tan Motel on the night of the murder, answered your description.

'It seemed this Richards was alone and didn't have a wife joining him or anybody who was passing as his wife, so the manager was a little bit curious and remembered exactly what this man looked like. So when the police wanted to know if there was anything unusual that had happened there the night of the murder, she remembered you being there without a wife. Anyway this man, Sellers, knew you had registered there.'

'Go on,' I said.

'Well, Banks saw those wires going through and thought that you were planning to stay there with this girl who works for him. Her name was . . . wait a minute . . . honestly, Donald, I'm terrible on names.'

'Hines?' I asked.

'That's it,' she said. 'Hines. I remember her first name was May. He kept referring to her as May. Well, it seems he went down there sort of snooping around, and the first thing he ran on to was me doing a strip tease in front of the window – only, of course, he didn't know it was a strip tease. It was just a good-looking woman undressing as far as he was concerned, and – Well, anyway, that's his story.'

'Did the police buy that story?'

'Honestly, I don't know. They got his story and then they rushed him out of there fast.'

'They didn't ask you any questions?'

'No. Told me to pull my shades down and thanked me for being sufficiently cool to keep on undressing after I'd called the police. They said that was a wonderful thing to do and asked me how I happened to think of it and I told them that I thought that was the only way I could be sure of holding the man there until the police arrived.'

'Was this police officer, Sellers, there?' I asked.

'Was he there!' she exclaimed. 'I'll say he was there. He telephoned to someone – Donald, have you got a partner, a woman by the name of . . . wait a minute, it's the same as a cigarette, a . . . Cool. That's the name. *C-o-o-l.*'

'Yes. Why?'

'Sellers telephoned her, and boy, did he read her a riot act! He told her that he'd protected you for her sake as long as he was going to, that this was the end. You're a detective, aren't you, Donald?'

'Uh-huh.'

'I knew there was something phony about your approach,' she said, 'but you bought me food and built up my morale. Boy, I certainly was low when you showed up on the scene. I was so low I could reach up and touch bottom. Honestly, Donald, I was even thinking of taking sleeping pills – only I didn't have the pills. *Now* I'm a normal woman, well fed and purring like a cat.'

She started humming a little tune and reached for the zipper on her dress, her hips keeping time to the tune she was humming.

'Look at me,' she said. 'Every time I start stripping I get sort of all worked up. Donald, this is the tune I used to work to. I'd move in rhythm with the music, like this – and then I'd start peeling while I was walking. I'd have a tantalizing little smile on my face – like I knew I was going to do something very naughty but just didn't care.

'Then I'd pull the zipper a few inches and then hesitate – like this – and act as if maybe I'd changed my mind. Then I'd get the daring smile back and pull the zipper –'

I picked up the telephone and told the operator: 'I want to get Colley Norfolk,' and gave her Norfolk's night number.

Publicity was siren music to the ears of the stripper, and she quit pulling the zipper to listen.

When I had Colley on the line, I said: 'Okay, Colley, your idea worked.'

'What the hell are you talking about?' he asked.

'Don't be a goof,' I said. 'The idea of planting your stripper in a motel and have her catch the Peeping Tom the police have been trying to nail in connection with a murder.'

'Hot dog!' Colley said. 'Did it work?'

'It worked.'

'Where's the guy now?'

'At police headquarters, presumably, but they probably won't let anyone know it for a while.'

'Where's the broad?' he asked.

'With me.'

'Where are you?'

I gave him the room number in the hotel. 'Round up some reporters and get down here right away,' I said.

'Be your age, Lam,' he said. 'I'll have a hard time getting them to print this, even if I furnish them with pictures of the girl doing her strip. They sure as hell aren't going to come all the way down to the beach to –'

'Grow up,' I told him. 'This is murder! The Peeping Tom is the key figure in a red-hot murder case. Police are going to keep him buried until they get all his story and round up some other witnesses and check out all the angles.

'You're going to be giving the newspapers a hot tip on something that's newsworthy, something that's tied into a murder case, and you've got headlines that make for the front page. PROFESSIONAL STRIPPER UNDRESSES IN FRONT OF WINDOW WHILE POLICE NAB PEEPING MURDER SUSPECT IN –'

'Good God,' he said, 'I never thought of that.'

'Think of it now,' I told him.

'Give me that address where you are once more,' he said.

I told him the name of the hotel and gave him the room number.

'Oh, God, what a break!' he exclaimed. 'This will put her on the map and give me the biggest boost for a publicity gag –'

'They'll want pictures of her in the motel,' I said.

'Pictures showing where the man was standing and showing just what he saw through the window, and you'll want a nice story for your client to give to the reporters about how the stripper doesn't mind if people look at her because that's her business, but she knows how the ordinary woman feels when strange masculine eyes look lustfully at her during moments of privacy.

'So this brave little woman decided to trap the man who had been –'

'Hell's bells!' he screamed into the phone, 'you don't have to do *all* my thinking for me.'

'I'm glad you told me,' I said.

'Cut the comedy,' he said. 'This is the story of a life-time. Boy, can I parlay this into publicity! Photographs right through the window – a stripping scene in front of a fireplace. Bra, panties and publicity. Sex, seduction and sure-fire story stuff. Get the hell off the line so I can start calling the newspapers!'

I hung up and said: 'Well, everything's working out fine. They're on their way down.'

'How long will it be before they can get here?' she asked.

'Before he gets them rounded up and gets the men on the job, before he can convince them that it's genuine publicity and not a phony deal, it'll probably be . . . oh, it'll probably be an hour to an hour and a half before they get here.'

She started humming the little tune and reached for the zipper on her dress once more.

'And,' I said, 'by the time they get here they'll find you here alone. I'll be long gone.'

'Donald,' she said reproachfully.

'I'm taking a powder right now.'

She said: 'I guess you weren't very interested in what you saw.'

'I was interested,' I told her. 'but I'm busy.'

'I'm grateful, Donald. I . . . I fell for you right from the start. I'm just in the mood to pitch a little woo. I guess it's the food and all the excitement and things. I . . . I feel sexy as hell.'

'I thought you strippers maintained an impersonal attitude,' I said, 'and thought only of your audience.'

She giggled and said: 'Didn't you want me to think of the audience, Donald? I was thinking of you all the time I was standing up there. I didn't know you had such powerful binoculars. I was afraid you might be disappointed, and –'

'Thanks,' I interrupted.

'What do you mean, thanks? Oh, for what I showed you?'

'For mentioning the binoculars,' I said. 'I'm taking them. Now look, Angel Eyes. You get this straight. Colley Norfolk was the one who originated this whole idea. If anyone asks you about Donald Lam, you have met him and that's all. But the whole idea of this thing was Colley Norfolk's.

'Remember that. Norfolk is a professional publicity man. He knows the ropes. He's in a position to cash in on this publicity you're going to get. You don't want to hurt his feelings. You want to let him know that you're grateful.'

'Listen, Donald, I'm not dumb. He'll *know* I'm grateful – and I *am* grateful. I know which side of the bread has the butter. But that's business. This is something else, Donald. The way I feel towards you, I –'

'You can best show your gratitude,' I said, 'by not

mentioning my name. Later on, if the police question you, that's different. Youre going to have to tell them the story. Otherwise you'll be out on a limb. But when you tell the police the story, be sure that you build it up so that you can get a second shot at more publicity.'

'They'll take pictures of me undressing over at the motel?' she asked.

'They'll take pictures,' I said. 'You can put on just as much of an act as you want, only they'll probably be in a hurry because once they realize the sort of story they have, their editors will be waiting for the art work to hit the front page.'

'Hot dog!' she said. 'Boy, I just feel full of curves.'

'Keep feeling that way,' I told her. 'It will make your performance go over that much bigger. Now, wait here for the reporters.'

She walked over to the window and stood looking over towards the motel again. She started humming the little tune. Her hips were swaying with the seductive rhythm of a professional stripper. She reached almost mechanically for the half-pulled zipper at the back of her dress and slid it all the way down.

I took the binoculars and eased out of the door, closed it silently behind me and hurried down the corridor.

Chapter 14

It was nearly midnight when I drove my rented car into Banning.

I didn't want to take chances with the police right at the moment, but there was no other way I knew of getting what I wanted. On pins and needles lest I should be picked up as a prowler, I drove my car into the first motel I came to, made a complete circle, watching the cars and the licence numbers, and then drove out. I repeated the performance on the second one. It was at the third motel that I struck pay dirt. The Chevrolet with licence number RTD 671 was parked in front of Cabin number 10.

There was one last vacancy in the motel, so I was able to rent a unit and park my car. After the manager had switched on the electric sign announcing there were no more vacancies and had gone to bed, I walked over to Cabin number 10 and knocked gently at the door.

Once again luck was with me. Irene evidently wasn't sleeping. I heard her moving around on the bed, then her feet on the floor, and her voice, sharp with tension, saying: 'Who is it?'

'Donald,' I said.

She opened the door a crack.

'Donald,' she said, 'I'm in my nightie. I –'

'Got a robe?' I asked.

'No, I haven't. I –'

'Take a blanket,' I said in a half whisper. 'Throw it around you. I've got to see you, fast.'

'Just a minute.'

She went to the bed, then a moment later was back with a blanket wrapped around her.

'Don't switch on the light,' I told her in a half whisper.

I went in and closed the door behind me.

'The walls are terribly thin,' she whispered. 'People will know that . . . that I'm having a visitor.'

'That's all right,' I told her. 'People have probably been wondering about you ever since you registered by yourself, and you don't want to disappoint them. Have you seen the papers?'

'Yes.'

'There'll be some more stuff in tomorrow's papers,' I said. 'You'll find that the police are looking for me.'

'For *you*?'

'That's right,' I said. 'Keep your voice down.'

'But why are they looking for you?'

'It had to be one or the other of us,' I said. 'I either had to come forward and tell the police about you or else keep in the background and let them find out about me the hard way.'

'But how could they find out about you?'

'You'll read it in the papers,' I told her. 'I haven't time to discuss it now. I notice from the newspaper account that Dowling left no immediate relatives.'

'I read that.'

'Know anything about it?'

'No. I know that he was very lonely and sometimes he

had mentioned to me that he had no near relatives.'

'There will be cousins, nephews and what-have-you,' I said.

'What do you mean, Donald? What – Why should you get me up in the night to talk that over with me?'

She was seated on the edge of the bed, and enough light came through the window so I could see the drawn, anxious lines of her face.

'Figure it out,' I told her. 'Your son is Herbert Dowling's son; illegitimate, of course, but nevertheless a blood relative.'

She gasped. 'Donald, do you mean that would . . . that would make any difference?'

'It could make a lot of difference,' I said, 'depending on various and sundry matters of proof.

'It will make a difference to you, it would make a difference to your son, and it would make one whale of a difference to the collateral relatives who would fight tooth and nail in order to get their places aboard the gravy train.'

'You mean they'd drag me into it, and my son?'

'Hell's bells,' I said, 'be your age! They'd drag you into it and cut you to pieces. They'll try to make out a perfect case of murder against you. They'll make a black-mailer out of you and claim that you had victimized Dowling into believing he was the father of your son – in short, Irene, the party's going to get rough.'

She sat there on the bed, the blanket wrapped around her, thinking things over.

'Is there anything, anything on earth I can do?' she asked.

'Lots,' I said.

'Can you help, Donald?'

'I'm trying to help now,' I said. 'I'm taking risks. As long as I can keep out of the clutches of the police, I can keep stirring things up. The minute they grab me, I'm out of circulation and can't do a thing.

'Now then, I want some help.'

'What?'

I said: 'You kept track of Dowling. You kept up with what he was doing. When he saw you, he evidently confided in you.

'You understood him and he knew it. You understood his problems. You sympathized with him. Presumably you were still pretty much in love with him, yet you wouldn't go back to the old relationship. After you became a mother, you felt you had a responsibility to your son. You wanted him brought up right.

'Now then, you know a lot about Dowling which perhaps other people don't know. He has from time to time had surreptitious meetings with a woman who presumably is working in his office. I want to know who she is.'

'Can you describe her?' she asked.

'She's somewhere between twenty-six and thirty-one. She has large, dark eyes, long eyelashes, and she has a rather peculiar walk; a seductive sway. It's not a wiggle. It's a rhythm. A –'

'Doris Gilman,' she interrupted.

'All right, what about her?'

'I knew that Herbert was . . . well, interested in her, but he's all tied up with Bernice Clinton. She's got some sort of a hold on him and – I just can't bring myself to speak of him in the past tense, Donald, it – You have to understand –'

'Never mind,' I interrupted. 'I understand all that. We

147

don't have any time for sentiment right now. We're trying to get facts and I have to have them fast. Tell me
about Doris Gilman.'

'She's something of an enigma. I don't know too much
about her or about her background. She's very close-
mouthed.

'I do know that Herbert took a friendly interest in
her, and I think she was advising him. I didn't know that
anything had . . . anything intimate had delevoped.'

'I didn't know that it had, either,' I said. 'Maybe it
hadn't. Do you know where I could find this woman?'

'No, I don't. I – It seems to me that I heard she was
– No, I'm sorry, Donald. I don't think I could help you.'

'All right,' I said, 'tell me this. Bernice Clinton is maintaining an apartment in Santa Ana under the name of
Agnes Dayton. It's a swank apartment. I suppose Dowling
was putting up the money for that.'

'In Santa Ana!' she exclaimed.

I nodded.

'Heavens, no,' she said. 'Dowling has an apartment
for her in Los Angeles.'

'Know the address?' I asked.

'I can't give you the street address,' she said, 'but it's
in the Regina Arms.'

'All right, here's one more question. Bernice Clinton
registered at the Swim and Tan Motel under the name
of Agnes Dayton. That's the same name that she uses in
the apartment in Santa Ana. Now, why did she register
at the Swim and Tan Motel?'

Irene shook her head. 'I wouldn't know, Donald.'

'Dowling met you there?'

'Yes.'

'Several times?'

'That was where we always met.'

'Then, if he wanted to meet with Bernice, do you think he'd –'

'Heavens, no!' she interposed. 'Why should he meet *her* there? He was maintaining an apartment for her in Los Angeles. Moreover, as far as Herbert was concerned, the affair had run its course. He was beginning to know her for what she was, a scheming gold-digger.

'I don't think he ever had been in love with her. He'd been infatuated by her and believe me, that girl plays everything she has to get what she wants. She's good at it. Herbert was lonely and just a little bit lost, and she came along and started flaunting her figure in front of his eyes and throwing herself at him, only she did it so cleverly that Herbert thought *he* was the one who was making the passes at *her*. It's . . . it's the same old story.'

I looked her over.

'Don't look at me like that, Donald,' she said. 'It wasn't that way with us. I . . . I loved him and he loved me, and if he could be alive to talk with you right today, he'd tell you that when I walked out of his life it left a great big vacuum that he could never fill.

'Those evenings that we had at the Swim and Tan Motel were . . . well, he looked forward to them far more than the surreptitious trysts he had with those other girls who were simply . . . well, where it was simply a . . . well, you know.'

I said: 'Okay, Irene. I just wanted to warn you. The thing has got to come out. Your son, Herbert, has got to come into the limelight. I'm sorry about it, but it can't be helped.'

'Donald, if they question me, what shall I tell them?'

'Say absolutely nothing,' I said, 'until you get an attorney. If he's any good, he'll tell you to keep quiet until after I've had a chance to dig out a few more facts. I'm on my way.'

'Donald, are you . . . are you in any danger?'

'Not unless I resist arrest,' I said, 'and I'm not foolish enough to do that, but I'll probably get a good working-over when they pick me up.'

'You mean they'll beat you up?'

'Frank Sellers,' I said, 'is inclined to get a little rough when he loses his temper, and I'm afraid he's lost his temper.'

'You poor boy,' she said, 'you're doing this for me. You're . . .'

The blanket dropped to the floor. Her arms were around me. Her eyes were looking steadily into mine. 'Donald,' she said, 'this isn't a pass. I just feel that you understand me and . . . that we understand each other. Thank you for what you're doing.'

She kissed me and opened the door.

I gave her a reassuring hug. 'Take it easy,' I told her. 'Try and get some sleep. Keep your chin up.'

I drove to Palm Springs, went into a phone booth and put through a long-distance call to Bertha Cool at her apartment.

It was a minute or two before I heard Bertha's sleepy voice on the telephone. 'Hello . . . hello – What the hell? . . . Who's calling at this time of night? You –'

'It's Donald,' I said.

'You!' Bertha screamed, her anger snapping her wide awake. 'You little bastard! You have *really* done it this time! You're finished. Frank Sellers will see you never

150

get another licence in this business as long as you live. You're –'

'Shut up and listen,' I told Bertha.

'Shut up and listen? Why, you little bastard! You upstart! You two-bit four-flushing double-crosser! Do you know what's going to happen to you?'

'What's going to happen to me?' I asked.

'You're going to be convicted of first-degree murder,' Bertha said. 'You've led with your chin. You've got Sellers sore, and nothing I can do is going to help you in the least. Sellers has tied you right in with that murder.'

'How nice,' I said. 'Has he found the murder weapon?'

'I don't know what the hell he's found,' Bertha said, 'but I do know he's got enough on you to put you into the gas chamber. I'll tell you something else. That Agnes Dayton, who saw the prowler at the motel, has identified your picture as that of the man she saw peering in at her.'

'The hell she has!' I exclaimed, unable to keep the surprise out of my voice.

'That's right,' Bertha said. 'Frank Sellers showed her your picture and she identified it instantly. Then there was Marcia Elwood, the woman who had just emerged from the shower, apparently only a few minutes after Dowling was murdered. She described you to a T and as soon as she saw your picture she told Sellers that was a photograph of the man she had seen watching her. She said she'd recognize you anywhere.

'Your goose is cooked, you little bastard. But what gets me is why the hell you shot this man. I don't know what you had against him. I told Frank Sellers that as far as I knew you'd never even met him, but that I did know you were working on him.'

151

I thought all that over for a moment.

'You there?' Bertha asked.

'I'm here.'

'Where the hell is here?'

'Palm Springs.'

'And what are you doing there?'

'Finding out who killed Herbert Dowling,' I said.

'Sellers has already found out,' she told me. 'You're the guy for his book.'

'He can't make it stick,' I said. 'Agnes Dayton gave an entirely different description of the man she saw peeping in the window.'

'Descriptions don't count as against a personal identification,' Bertha said. 'She's made an absolutely positive identification of your photograph, and Marcia Elwood is positive as hell.'

I said: 'That's the way police do things. They get a photograph and get a person to study it and implant the idea in the mind of that person that the photograph is that of the criminal. Then when the person sees that person in the line-up –'

'Oh, bunk!' Bertha interrupted. 'I've heard you yakkity-yak on that stuff so much.'

'Well, it works,' I said. 'The power of suggestion –'

'The power of suggestion, my eye!' Bertha snapped. 'You've got yourself in one hell of a mess.

'Now, you take my advice. You ring up Frank Sellers right now and apologize to him. You tell him that you're sorry you tried to hold out on him and tried to mastermind a murder case; that you're innocent; that you want to surrender and come clean.

'Maybe if you do that, I can bring enough influence to bear with him so that he won't press a charge of first-degree murder but will let you cop a plea on second degree.

'For God's sake, Donald, can't you see enough naked women on your own without going around prowling through back alleyways, looking in lighted windows and –'

'You're several paragraphs behind, Bertha,' I said. 'They've already caught the prowler, the Peeping Tom. He's Rossiter D. Banks. He's the manager of a branch office of the telegraph company and they caught him tonight.'

Bertha thought that over for a moment, then said: 'I haven't heard from Sellers – he's quit taking me into his confidence. Donald, you're too damn slick on these things. I have an idea you jockeyed that guy into some sort of a trap. Now, you get busy on the phone and tell Frank Sellers that you're coming in and surrender to him personally.'

'I'll think it over,' I told Bertha. 'And in the meantime I don't want to spend any more agency money on telephone bills and –'

'*Agency* money!' Bertha screamed. 'Why, listen, you little bastard, this has nothing to do with the agency. This is your individual trouble. You're in it and you can damn well get yourself out of it. Don't think that I'm going to pay for your telephone calls. Don't think that the agency – Agency, hell!'

I gently eased the receiver back into place and left the phone booth.

The Bonanza Airlines had an early plane to Phoenix.

The first of the Peeping Tom clippings showed the woman who had reported a prowler at the Swim and Tan Motel was Helen Corliss Hart of Phoenix; that she operated a beauty parlour and had been able to give the police a fairly good description of the prowler: a rather mature man with a long nose, bushy eyebrows and with an air of dignity; hardly the type of person one would expect to be a Peeping Tom.

I knew that within a few hours Frank Sellers would be showing her photographs of me, trying to make her believe I was the man she'd seen. He'd tell her that Agnes Dayton had made a positive identification; that Marcia Elwood had seen me there and that he knew I was the party she'd seen. He'd ask her to study my photograph and keep studying it. He'd point out that, after all, she was excited, that she'd only had a brief glimpse of the prowler's face and then she'd started to scream and had telephoned for the police. . . . It was the same old trick, the power of suggestion working on eye-witness identification.

My only hope was to confront Helen Hart in the flesh before Sellers could get to her with a photograph.

I looked through the telephone book. She had both a business address and an apartment address in Phoenix.

I put through a call.

It was a few minutes before I heard her voice, rather sleepy.

'Mrs Hart,' I said, 'or is it Miss Hart? I'm a detective, at present at Palm Springs, and – Is it Mrs Hart or is it Miss Hart?'

'My professional name is Helen Corliss Hart,' she said. 'I refer to myself as Miss. What is it you want, calling me at this hour of the night?'

I said: 'It's rather important. You saw a prowler at the Swim and Tan Motel a week or so ago. You reported the incident to the police. I think I can put my finger on the man if you can give me a little better description.'

'I can't give you any more than I gave the police when they interviewed me,' she said, 'and good heavens, if I'm to have my sleep broken up by –'

'It's very important, Miss Hart,' I said. 'I don't like to bother you but – Look, could you have breakfast with me?'

'Where did you say you were calling from?'

'I'm in Palm Springs.'

'That's what I thought you said.'

'I'll get a plane and if you could have breakfast with me, I would like to –'

'I'm a working woman,' she said. 'I have a beauty-shop that I have to keep operating and I have seven girls working under me. I don't have any time to fritter away and –'

'That's what I meant by asking you for breakfast,' I said. 'You could eat and talk.'

'I'm watching my figure,' she said. 'My breakfasts consist mostly of coffee.'

'Eight o'clock?' I asked.

'Heavens, no,' she said. 'Seven-thirty.'

'I'll be there on the dot.'

'You're a police detective?'

'Private,' I said, 'but I'm working on the case.'

'Well, you must be working if you – I *should* be angry at being called up but you sound earnest and sincere.'

'I am earnest and sincere. I'm also trying my darnedest to get this case solved. I'll see you at seven-thirty.'

'On the dot,' she said. 'I won't wait.'

'I'll be at your apartment. We can go out and –'

'No, you're having breakfast with me,' she said, 'provided you don't want anything more than coffee and Melba toast. I'm not going to cook for you.'

'I'll be there,' I told her. 'Bye now.'

'Bye,' she said, and her voice wasn't quite as edged with hostility. I could see that I had aroused her interest.

It would have helped if I could take my tape-recorder along so I could record the interview and her description of the Peeping Tom, but after all, the main thing was to beat Frank Sellers to the punch. By the time she'd had breakfast with me without raising any howl of protest, she'd have one hell of a time making a subsequent identification of me as the prowler.

Of course Sellers didn't absolutely need her identification, but I sure as hell needed to show the descriptions of the prowlers didn't agree.

What I couldn't understand was how it happened that Bernice Clinton, in as precarious a position as she was, living in Santa Ana under the name of Agnes Dayton, had had the nerve to identify *my* picture and not let on that she knew me as Donald Lam. It meant that she was in the thing up to her eyebrows and was taking a desperate gamble.

I wanted to look over what Montrose Carson was doing with his Palm Springs development and, while one-thirty in the morning wasn't the best time to look at real estate, I wanted to look things over. So I drove out to the place.

There is nothing quite as depressing as a high-power sales effort on which the power has been stalled to a standstill.

Seen in the small hours of the morning by the light of a gibbous moon, Montrose L. Carson's *Sage, Sand and Sun Sub-division* was dead-looking. All the gaudy bunting which surrounded the information booth was limp and dejected in the moonlight. The triangular flags which were supposed to dance gaily in the desert breeze, the colours brilliant in the sunshine, were drab, limp and lifeless in the still air of the quiet night.

Overhead the lopsided moon leered down from the sky. The stars were calm with the tranquillity of outer space. The acres of sage-studded sand swept away, silvery in the moonlight, splotched with black shadows and bathed in the brooding silence of the desert.

Behind the stretch of sand the towering slopes of San Jacinto Mountain rose more than two miles straight up in the air, a huge tumbled mass of granite spotted with snow and fringed with huge fir trees up above the granite.

The lights of Palm Springs were far to the west and north. Occasionally from the motor road could be heard the whine of tyres snarling along the highway.

I prowled the sub-division. Evidently Carson was doing all right for himself. Along the front row of lots a big majority had the red sign marked in bold letters 'SOLD'. Farther back there were not quite so many signs announcing that lots had been sold, but considering the fact the sub-division was only some thirty days old, it was doing all right for itself.

I stooped and picked up a brochure which some potential customer had discarded.

Even by the light of the lopsided moon I could tell that it was a classy job, printed on heavy glazed paper, a dozen pages of sales talk, statistics and photographs.

I thrust the brochure into my coat pocket, prowled around for a while, went back to the rented car and drove to the airport.

I found that I couldn't quite make connections by

taking the regular morning flight, which was all right with me because I was afraid Frank Sellers might have a representative on that plane.

I inquired about chartering a plane, and the attendant was glad to put through the call for me.

I talked with the pilot whom I had pulled out of bed but who seemed quite cheerful nevertheless. He made me a special price on one way to Phoenix and said he could be there within thirty minutes and ready to take off.

I settled down in the waiting-room and pulled the brochure out of my pocket.

It showed photographs of the main street of Palm Springs, the exclusive shops with merchandise catering to the wealthy tourist. It showed pictures of the shaded date groves of Indio. It gave statistics on winter temperature, the number of days of sunshine. And on the back was a portrait of the originator of this great enterprise, the benign countenance of Montrose Levining Carson; his eyes holding the reader in his most solemn, executive stare.

The photograph somehow gave the whole thing an air of complete stability and respectability.

I started to toss the whole thing into the waste-basket, then moved by some impulse, opened my knife and carefully cut out the picture of Montrose Carson.

A scheme was beginning to dawn in my mind that would make any trick I had ever pulled on Sergeant Frank Sellers of the Los Angeles Police Department look tame by comparison.

If he wanted to stack the cards against me, I'd show him something about card stacking.

My pilot showed up and soon had the plane out, ready

to go. Fortunately, he had a pad of scratch paper in the plane.

All the way to Phoenix I practised drawing crude pictures of Montrose Levining Carson. By the time we set down at Phoenix Airport, I had him down pat. I could knock off a sketch which was a fairly credible likeness.

I paid off the pilot, went into the men's room at the Phoenix Airport, tore all the sketches I had made and the original photograph of Carson into small pieces and flushed them down the toilet.

A taxi took me to the address of Helen Corliss Hart.

I looked at my watch. I was right on time. By spending the price of a private charter plane I had gained exactly thirty minutes on the time of the commercial airline.

Thinking how Bertha would feel at the price I had paid for those thirty minutes, I felt butterflies in my stomach.

Chapter 15

Helen Corliss Hart was attired in a smart tailored outfit. It was very difficult for a man to guess her age. A woman *might* have done it – and might have guessed wrong, at that.

She was a poised, sophisticated woman and she radiated feminine charm and appeal. It was a mature charm, not the post-adolescent appeal of the younger woman.

Helen Hart was tree-ripened fruit and you had the feeling that it would be a long time before the process of deterioration would begin.

She looked me over with appraising eyes, then smiled and gave me her hand.

'My name is Lam,' I said.

'Hello, Mr Lam,' she said. 'You're not the sort of person I expected.'

'What sort did you expect?'

'A big thick-necked, broad-shouldered man who would size me up and make passes on a take-it-for-granted basis, with a few coarse jokes about the view the Peeping Tom must have had.'

'And you don't think I'm that kind?'

'I'm sure you're not.

'You don't think I've tried to size you up?'

She said: 'Oh, come off of it – you've sized me up. You may make passes but they won't be on a take-it-for-granted basis. They'll be intriguing and interesting and therefore unobjectionable. Now, do you want your coffee black or with cream and sugar?'

'Cream and sugar, please,' I said.

She sighed. 'I don't know how it is people like you can indulge their every want and still wind up with a dimple for a stomach. Now, look at me, I –' She broke off, laughing. 'Well, don't look *that* hard! . . . What's your first name?'

'Donald.'

'All right, Donald. Let's get friendly. I don't have much time. We've got to cover a lot of ground. You want to ask me questions, I want to get to work. You want to get back to your business. Let's go.'

She led the way into a little kitchen where there was a breakfast nook and seated herself on one side. I seated myself across the table.

She said: 'There's a toaster here and bread. There isn't an ounce of butter in the place. I have Melba toast. If you want dry toast, you can have it. There aren't any eggs and I'm not going to cook for you.'

I said: 'All I want is coffee, Helen. Now, what I want to know is how good a look you got at that man's face.'

'I got a darn good look at it. It's etched on my memory.'

'You'd know him if you saw him again?'

'I certainly would.'

'Do you remember the description you gave to the police?'

'Yes, and I remember exactly what he looked like.'

I said: 'I'm something of an artist. Let's start with hair.'

'He had a hat on.'

'All right, what about the eyes? Glasses?'

'No glasses.'

'What colour?'

'A light colour, but the big thing about the eyes were the eyebrows. There was something about the eyebrows that I can't describe so anyone else would know what it was, but it was distinctive.'

'Nose?'

'A long, straight nose.'

I said: 'Let me do a little sketching. I've studied the description you gave the police. Let's see if I can make a sketch of the face.'

I made a somewhat distorted sketch of the face of Montrose Carson.

'The eyes are too far apart,' she said.

I made another sketch, putting the eyes closer together.

'The eyebrows are too arched. This man had straighter eyebrows, and there's something about the mouth. You have the corners of the mouth turning up. This man had a straight mouth.'

'Cheek-bones?'

'High cheek-bones – You're getting it now, Donald . . . Donald, you're getting it! That's almost him. That's a darn good sketch. Donald, you're a genius with a pencil.'

I said modestly: 'I was just following your description.'

'Donald, that's good. It's so good I'm afraid of it.'

'What do you mean, afraid of it?'

'Well, you've taken the features that I described to you and moulded them into a composite sketch that looks so natural I'd identify that sketch. And yet . . . I don't know. I suppose there's a certain element of suggestion that enters into the situation.

'When I first looked at your sketch, I thought it was a good sketch. Now, the more I look at it, the more I think it's a rough portrait of the man himself. I know that some of that is auto-suggestion. I look at the various features and then see them all combined and . . . well, I get self-hypnotized.'

'But if you've described the features accurately and if that sketch is an accurate reproduction, there's nothing to worry about.'

'I know, but –'

I interrupted to say: 'You're sure of your description? It couldn't have been . . . couldn't have been *me*, for instance?'

She laughed and said: 'Don't be a goose, Donald! I imagine that whenever you want to see a woman undress you don't have to stand *outside* the window.'

'This man looked the frustrated type?'

'Well, not exactly. It's hard to describe. Donald, I don't suppose you ever could understand my feelings unless you were a woman.'

'I'm not,' I said.

'I'm quite certain you're not. . . . I suppose that a woman who has a good figure likes to show it under proper circumstances, but when you think you have privacy and step out into a lighted apartment, and then suddenly see a man's face staring at you from the darkness of a window . . .'

'You screamed?'

'I screamed,' she said, 'and tried to grab something to cover myself and then I rushed for the phone and called the police.'

'And the man?'

'The man turned and I could see him running for a few steps and then I lost sight of him in the darkness outside the window.'

'Then what did you do?'

'I dashed over and pulled the shade. . . . You know, Donald, that was a most peculiar design for a motel room. It's in the form of a big L, with this back window where you'd least expect it. The bathroom takes a corner of the room and then when you step out – well, you suddenly realize you're right in front of a window and you just didn't notice that window or know it existed before.'

'Probably it was built that way for cross-ventilation,' I said.

'Undoubtedly. But most motels have the back side so constructed there's a frosted glass window in the bathroom, a window too small for anybody to crawl into, and frosted so that no one can see into it. Aside from that, there isn't any window in the back end.'

'Do you have any idea how long this man had been there?'

'No, I haven't. And – gosh, I guess I was real careless. I wanted to go out to dinner. I'd been driving and was anxious to climb into a hot shower. I just opened the suitcase, got out some fresh clothes, climbed out of my clothes and walked into the shower.'

'Robe?' I asked.

'Don't be silly,' she said. 'I was in a hurry. I wanted to go out to dinner and I really wanted that shower. I walked around that apartment just as naked as the day I was born, and then I came out and saw this man staring at me. It – I don't know, it makes you sort of sick to your stomach.'

'To have men staring like that?'

'Don't be silly, Donald. Men have seen me without clothes on, but it's been by invitation. This man was just . . . well, leering.'

'How was his size, compared with mine?'

'Well, of course I didn't see all of him, but from the way he stood at the window and what I saw of him when he ran, I would say he was older than you and bigger; that is, both taller and broader. He . . .'

The chimes sounded.

She frowned. 'Now, who in the world can that be at this hour in the morning?' She looked at her wrist-watch and said: 'I've got to get the shop opened up – excuse me a moment, will you, Donald?'

I sat there in the breakfast alcove, heard her go to the door and heard the voice of Frank Sellers saying: 'Excuse me, ma'am. I don't like to intrude on you in the morning this way, but I'm Frank Sellers of the Los Angeles Police and this is Sergeant Ransom of the Phœnix Police Department. We'd like to talk with you for a few minutes.'

'Well,' she said, 'I'm terribly busy at the moment and –

'If you'd just spare us a few minutes,' Sellers said, and walked in.

The other voice, that I assumed was that of Sergeant Ransom, said: 'I know you're very busy, Miss Hart, but this may clear up rather an important crime.'

'What in the world would I know that – Oh, that Peeping Tom business?'

'Exactly,' Frank Sellers said.

'We think we know the man that's responsible. We've had him positively identified by the other victims, and if we can just get *your* identification, it will close the case. Then you can rest assured that other women won't have to be subjected to the annoying experience that you had.

'Now, this fellow is a pretty slick operator. He's a

F*

smooth customer. . . . Here's his picture, he . . .'

There was a moment of silence, the rustle of papers.

'Good heavens!' Helen Hart screamed. 'That's not the Peeping Tom! That's the detective who's . . .'

'Who is where?' Ransom asked coldly as she bit her words off.

I heard Sellers start moving.

'In . . . in the kitchenette,' Helen Hart said.

They hit the door with shattering force. Sellers was first. He lunged across the table, grabbed a handful of my shirt and collar, jerked me up off the bench and said: 'So, you smart little sonofabitch, you thought you could cover your tracks, eh?'

Helen Hart screamed: 'Don't touch him.'

'He's resisting arrest,' Sellers said, and hit me so hard on the chin that my head rocked back against the wall. The room spun into a weird merry-go-round, and I felt myself being sucked down into black oblivion.

When I regained consciousness, there were handcuffs on my wrists and Helen Hart was mad, talking a mile a minute.

'I don't know what you're trying to do. I've heard about police brutality. This is the first instance I've experienced. You struck a defenceless man.

'All he was trying to do was find out the person who really was the Peeping Tom, and he listened to my description and drew an absolutely one hundred per cent accurate sketch, a sketch that I could identify.'

'Where is it?' Ransom asked.

'There are several sketches,' she said. 'He was trying to get an idea of what the man looked like from my description, and he kept drawing sketches. Here's the whole set of them and here's the finished sketch.'

'Phooey!' Sergeant Sellers said. 'This guy was selling you a bill of goods. *He* was the Peeping Tom. He came on here and started handing you a line of hooey so that you'd think it was someone else. We've got this guy dead to rights. We've got an absolutely positive identification and we've got motivation. We've got him tied with a murder.'

'You haven't got him tied in with anything,' Helen Hart said. 'I'm going to protest this sort of brutality. I –'

'Now listen, Miss Hart,' Ransom said placatingly. 'You don't understand the risks a police officer takes. When he's making an arrest of this sort he gets so he can read a person's mind. This man was getting ready to slug Sellers and –'

'Getting ready to slug Sellers, my eye!' she stormed. 'He was sitting there. . . . Why, he couldn't have slugged this big bruiser in a hundred years. If he'd hit that officer with his fist, he'd have broken his arm. Don't tell me what was happening. I saw it. I saw it with my own eyes.'

'You didn't get in here until later,' Ransom said.

'Don't hand me that line,' she said. 'I may be dependent on police protection, but I'm a taxpayer here and I'm going to stand up for what's fair and square.'

'Well,' Sergeant Ransom said, 'I'm sorry it happened. Perhaps Sellers was a little hasty. He's been up all night working on this case, and this character, Lam, has given him a bad time.'

'I'll say he's given me a bad time,' Sellers said. 'He's concealed evidence, he's obscured evidence, he's doctored evidence, he's twisted things around so that he's got everything all backwards – and that includes you, young lady. Don't tell me that he didn't sell you a bill of goods. He's an attractive guy and he sure knows how to sell himself to the ladies.'

'He didn't sell,' Helen Hart said, 'I bought. And I'm sticking up for him.'

Ransom noticed my open eyes and said dryly: 'We've got company, Sergeant.'

Sellers looked at me. For a moment I saw blind, unreasoning anger in his eyes. He wanted to hit me again.

Ransom read his mind and said: 'We'll let Miss Hart get on with her business and we'll take this man down to headquarters for further questioning.'

Helen Hart said: 'All right. I'm going to have my attorney look into the matter. I'm going to make it my business to see if your "further questioning" consists of any further police brutality. You lay a finger on him and we'll have an investigation here in Phœnix that will make a shake-up all the way along the line.'

'Now, there's no need for you to get excited or get to feeling partisan about this,' Ransom said.

Sellers jerked on the handcuffs. 'Come on, Pint Size,' he said. 'You're going places.'

Sellers hustled me out of the apartment while Helen Hart started for the telephone.

'You just sit tight, Donald,' she said. 'I'm going to have my own lawyer look into this situation . . . and he's a darn good lawyer.'

Chapter 16

The room at headquarters was typical. Battered oak furniture, a linoleum floor which at first glance seemed to be covered with caterpillars, each of the caterpillars a burnt streak made by carelessly tossed cigarettes. The chairs were straight-backed, stiff, uncomfortable, but solid and substantial. The furniture went back to a day when things were built to last, and because the furniture had lasted it had never been replaced.

It was a room where style and comfort meant nothing. It had been designed for utility and it had seen years of service.

Frank Sellers kicked the door shut. A spring lock clicked into position.

Sellers turned to me. 'Now, you double-crossing little sonofabitch, we're going to get at the bottom of this and we're going to get at it damn fast.'

Ransom wasn't quite so optimistic and a lot more cautious. 'Now look, Frank,' he said, 'this Helen Hart is dynamite. I know her lawyer. He's hell on wheels. If she gets the one I think she's going to get, we're in for a time.'

Sellers looked at me, frowned, and turned to Ransom. 'By the time her lawyer gets here,' he said, 'we'll have this guy all sewed up.'

Ransom shook his head.

I said: 'You aren't going to sew anybody up, Frank.
You're in Arizona now. You're not in your own baili-
wick. You aren't even a police officer here. You had no
right putting a finger on me. You couldn't even make an
arrest. You slugged me, and I'm going to see that you're
arrested for that slugging. I've got witnesses.

'What's more, you aren't going to get me anywhere
out of Arizona until you've got extradition, and I'm
going to resist extradition and demand a hearing.'

'See what I mean?' Ransom said.

Sellers came walking towards me. 'You double-crossing, pint-sized bastard!' he said, 'I'll show you whether
I've got any authority or –'

Knuckles sounded on the door.

At the second knock, Sergeant Ransom opened the
door a cautious crack.

A man's voice said: 'Party on the phone for you,
Sergeant. I think it's important.'

'Who is it?' Ransom asked.

'Moxey Malone.'

'Tell him I'll call him back,' Sergeant Ransom said.
'I'm busy now.'

'Okay, Sergeant.'

The door closed.

Ransom shook his head at Sellers. 'That does it,' he
said. 'Moxey Malone is the one I thought she'd get.'

'Who's he?'

'He's an attorney, and a smart one. What's more, he's
got an in with the governor.'

'What the hell's the governor got to do with it?'
Sellers asked.

'You heard what Lam said, Sergeant,' Ransom commented. 'You're in Arizona. You'll have to resort to extradition.'

Sellers's face darkened. 'By the time I get done with this guy he'll be waiving extradition and going back to Los Angeles and damn glad to go there.'

'Not in this state, not in this city, not in this jail and not while I'm here,' Ransom said. 'I live here, you don't.'

'Now, wait a minute,' Sellers said, 'we're not doing this case any good, talking in front of this guy.'

'All right, let's go talk someplace else,' Ransom said. 'The words are going to be the same.'

Sellers lurched towards the door, said over his shoulder: 'You wait there, Pint Size.'

'Take these handcuffs off,' I said. 'They're too tight. The bones of my wrists are hurting.'

'Now, ain't that too bad,' Sellers said, and opened the door and walked out.

Ransom looked at Sellers, then turned to look at me, said not unkindly: 'We won't be too long,' and walked out.

The door clicked shut.

I sat there for half an hour. When Sellers and Ransom came back, there was a third man with them, a short, thick-set, competent-looking man who had weight and knew how to throw it around.

'Hello, Lam,' he said. 'I'm Moxey Malone. I'm a lawyer. Your friend, Helen Corliss Hart, got me to represent you. They're holding you for the Los Angeles authorities on a warrant, suspicion of murder. Sit tight, say nothing. Don't even give them the time of day. The governor's secretary on criminal matters, including extradition, has set an informal hearing for tomorrow at ten o'clock.

'It's murder, and I can't get you bailed out before then. You're going to have to stay in the cooler until tomorrow morning. Don't be afraid. Nobody's going to hurt you. No matter what they *say*, they aren't going to *do* a damn thing.

'You'll get a square deal. The governor isn't going to extradite you unless they've got a case.'

Sellers said: 'We've got a case that'll surprise you. I hate to show my hand, but if I have to, I'll show it.'

'All right, go ahead and show it,' Malone said to him, 'but keep your hands off this guy.'

'Says who?' Sellers asked, turning on him belligerently.

'Says I,' Malone said, squaring up to him. 'And if you've got any friends here who have property, you'd better get them lined up because in about thirty minutes a warrant of arrest is going to be served on you for aggravated assault, grabbing Donald Lam when he was sitting at a table in an apartment and knocking him unconscious. You smashed his face with your fist and knocked his head against the wall. You can post bail and get out, but it'll be a good heavy bail. Then when I find out the extent of Lam's injuries, we're going to file a civil suit against you for ten thousand bucks. Hit him again and we'll make it twenty thousand with fifty thousand for exemplary damages.'

Sellers's face got purple. 'Why, you . . . you –'

'Take it easy. Take it easy,' Ransom warned.

'Go right ahead,' Malone invited.

Ransom said: 'This guy was a champion boxer in college, Sergeant. Take it easy.'

For two or three seconds Sellers and Malone stood glaring at each other. Then Sellers turned contemptuously on his heel and said: 'Okay, that's that.' He took two steps, turned back to Malone and said: 'Come to Los Angeles sometime, when you feel lucky.'

'I've been there,' Malone said. 'I don't like it. Do you make a habit of manhandling prisoners?'

'No, we don't make a habit of manhandling prisoners,' Sellers said. 'You don't know the facts in this case. I've given this little shrimp all the breaks in the world. He's double-crossed me. But we don't let lawyers bust in and tell us what to do. We've got a gymnasium out there if you think you'd like to do a little sparring.'

Malone's face broke into a grin. 'Now, isn't that just dandy,' he said. 'It just happens they've got a hell of a good gymnasium here. Come on, let's go down. I haven't had a work-out for a while.'

Ransom said: 'Nix, Sellers. Nix.'

Sellers stalked out of the room. Half a second later Ransom followed in a hurry. I said to Malone: 'Get a brochure of The Sage, Sand and Sun Sub-division out of Palm Springs. Telephone for it. Get it by plane—'

The door was jerked open. Ransom said: 'Right this way, Malone. *I'm* handling this.'

They went out. The door clicked shut.

Ten minutes later Ransom was back. He unlocked the handcuffs, said: 'Come on with me, Lam.'

They took me to the jail and booked me. I sat in a cell all that afternoon. I got fitful snatches of sleep during the night and at seven o'clock the next morning the jailer loaned me a razor. At nine-thirty I was put in an automobile. At ten o'clock I was sitting in a big, high-ceilinged room that was fitted up something like a small court-room.

Five minutes later a fellow in his early thirties came walking briskly into the room, carrying a brief-case. He climbed up behind the elevated desk and sat down. A door opened, and Sergeant Sellers came in; Bernice Clinton came in; Moxey Malone entered, and then Helen Corliss Hart came in and smiled reassuringly at me where I sat beside a big uniformed officer.

'All right,' the man behind the desk said. 'Let's go.'

He faced me and said: 'I'm Harvey C. Fillmore, the governor's pardoning secretary, and secretary in charge of extradition. I have been told the case against you is a frame-up. We don't ordinarily investigate evidence, but this time we're going to do it.

'Now then, gentlemen, let's hear what the case is against this prisoner. This is an informal hearing. I believe you want to present your case, Sergeant Sellers?'

Sellers got up.

'Just to keep the record straight,' Fillmore said, 'your name is Frank Sellers and you're a sergeant on the Los Angeles Police Force. Right?'

'Right,' Sellers said.

'All right. What's your case?'

Sellers said: 'Herbert Jason Dowling was murdered at the Swim and Tan Motel down at the beach. The indications are that he was killed by someone who was prowling the place, trying to get evidence. Dowling caught him in the act, and the guy smoked his way out.'

Fillmore said: 'What about proof?'

'We've got it,' Sellers said. 'I have a witness here who will identify this defendant, Donald Lam, as being the prowler she saw playing Peeping Tom while she was undressing. Dowling's car was at the motel and it had been bugged with an electronic shadowing device. We've traced that electronic shadowing device to Lam here. Lam dashed up to San Francisco and bought a new device so he could replace the part that was still clamped to Dowling's automobile. We caught him at it.

'What's more, we have a witness in California who couldn't be here today but who has given me an affidavit. She saw this prisoner, Donald Lam, peering at her window at this same motel the night of the murder and apparently only a few minutes after Dowling was killed. She makes a positive identification from a photograph.

'Dowling was killed with a twenty-two-calibre automatic. We found that automatic concealed in an apartment Donald Lam had been occupying. He's a licenced private detective, and the firm name is Cool and Lam.

'Do you want any more?'

'There's no need to get belligerent about it, Sergeant,' Fillmore said. 'I don't want any more. If you've got that, that's all you need to get a writ of extradition.'

Moxey Malone got up and said: 'If the Secretary pleases, I'd like to present a witness.'

'Let Sergeant Sellers get done first,' Fillmore said. 'Just for the sake of the record, will you make that same statement under oath, Sergeant?'

Frank Sellers held up his right hand and was sworn. 'I repeat that statement,' he said, 'every word of it. It's true.'

'You want to ask any questions?' Fillmore asked me.

Moxey Malone said: 'I'll represent the defendant, Mr Secretary.'

'Are there any questions?' Fillmore asked.

'Ask him about just where that gun was found,' I said.

Sellers said: 'We found it back of a hi-fi that was, in turn, concealed behind a set of dummy books. The book covers folded back like an accordion and disclosed the hi-fi set. The gun was in back of that hi-fi set.'

175

'It was the murder gun?' I asked.

'It was the murder gun,' Sellers said.

'You're under oath, Sergeant,' Fillmore said.

'I'm under oath,' Sellers said. 'The gun was tested by ballistics. It's the murder gun.'

'I guess that does it,' Fillmore said to Malone. 'This is an informal hearing, but I'm trying to expedite matters. We want to be fair.'

'I'd like to call a witness,' Malone said.

'You finished, Sergeant?' Fillmore asked.

'I'm finished,' Sellers said grimly.

I said: 'The sergeant said he had a witness who would testify that I was prowling the place.'

'She's right here,' Sellers said. 'Bernice Clinton.'

'I'd like to hear her statement under oath,' I said.

'If they've found the gun, you don't really need her statement,' Fillmore said.

I said: 'Let's assume she's made that statement. I'd like to ask her a couple of questions.'

Malone said in an undertone: 'Can you handle this, Lam?'

'I'll handle it,' I said.

Malone said: 'We'll stipulate that this witness would have made the statements Sellers said she would make, provided she is sworn and agrees that his statement was correct. Then my client wants to ask her some questions.'

'You or your client?' Fillmore asked.

'My client,' Malone said.

'When a man's represented by an attorney, the attorney is supposed to speak for him,' Fillmore said.

'This is informal,' Malone said. 'I haven't been in the case very long.'

'All right,' Fillmore said. 'We're trying to get at the bottom of the thing. Where's Bernice Clinton? Let her stand up and hold up her right hand.'

Bernice Clinton stood up, held up her right hand and was sworn.

'You've heard what Sergeant Sellers said about your testimony?' Fillmore asked.

'I have.'

'Would that be your testimony?'

'That would be my testimony.'

'You come up here and sit down where the accused can ask you some questions,' Fillmore said, not unkindly, sizing up Bernice Clinton's trim figure.

She came up and sat on the witness-stand.

I said: 'You recognize me as the man you saw looking in the window while you were undressing?'

'I do,' she said firmly.

I said: 'When did you next see me after that?'

She said: 'I saw you in Los Angeles and then I saw you in Santa Ana when you came to my apartment at the Corinthian Arms.'

'What's the name under which you rent that apartment?'

'Now, just a minute,' Frank Sellers said. 'Let's not let him start trying to drag her name through the mud. This is just a hearing to decide whether there's grounds for extradition. He can try all that smearing stuff when he gets her in court. It doesn't make any difference what name she rents the apartment under.'

'I think that's right,' Fillmore said. 'Ask her about the identification.'

I said: 'Didn't you negotiate with me for leasing a corner lot that I own?'

'I did.'

'And saw me several times in that connection?'

'Yes.'

'That was after you had had your experience at the Swim and Tan Motel and before you saw me in Santa Ana?'

'Yes.'

'And at those times you didn't recognize me as the man you had seen peering in the house?'

'No, I didn't. I was trying to get a lease from you and simply didn't think of you in that connection. It wasn't until after I had had a chance to think of you in connection with the prowler that I placed you. I knew I had seen your face somewhere before, but I couldn't tell where it was. I simply didn't associate you with that episode at the Swim and Tan Motel.'

'You didn't make that association until after Sergeant Sellers told you I was the person, did you?'

'He asked me.'

'And then you told him.'

'Then I knew where it was that I'd seen you before.'

'Whom were you representing in negotiating the lease for me?'

'Herbert Jason Dowling.'

'That was the dead man?'

'Yes.'

'I don't think we need to go into all this,' Fillmore said. 'If they have the murder weapon and it was found in your apartment, Mr Lam, it seems to me the governor is going to have to issue extradition.'

'We've got a witness we want to put on the stand,' Malone said.

'Who's that?'

'A local citizen, Helen Corliss Hart. She operates a beauty-shop here. She was one of the victims at the motel. The Peeping Tom looked in on her when she was emerging from the shower.'

'It doesn't make any difference,' Fillmore said. 'There might have been half a dozen Peeping Toms.'

'There has been an element of police brutality in the case,' Malone said.

'Arizona police?'

'No.'

'Who?'

'Sergeant Sellers.'

'He's not a police officer in this state. He's here as a private citizen,' Fillmore said. 'If you have any complaint against him, you have recourse to law.'

Sellers said: 'I've been arrested and am out on two-thousand-dollar bond.'

'I think that covers it,' Fillmore said.

I said: 'I was making sketches of the person Miss Hart saw looking in the window, using her description of the man's features and making a sketch. I made a sketch that looked pretty good. She said the sketch was a perfect likeness. I'd like to know what happened to those sketches. Did the police take them from her?'

'They did not,' Helen Hart said. 'I have them here.'

'Could I have them?'

'What good are they going to do?' Fillmore asked. 'I'm willing to concede for the sake of this hearing that there were half a dozen Peeping Toms. If you were there once and this witness, Bernice Clinton, says you were, that's all that's necessary as far as this hearing's concerned. Even without that, the possession of the murder weapon is sufficient for extradition.'

I said: 'If the Secretary pleases, I hadn't finished my questioning of this witness, Bernice Clinton.'

'I thought you had.'

'I beg your pardon, I hadn't. I had carried it to a certain point where you interposed and said that her testimony, with the finding of the gun in my apartment, was all that was needed.'

'Well, that's right. It is all that's needed.'

'I'd like to ask her a couple more questions.'

'We haven't all morning to devote to this matter. I'm only trying to find if there's a reasonable cause for the governor to grant extradition. It's an informal hearing, although I'm having the witnesses take oaths and am making a record. I'm satisfied right now.'

'I understand that,' I said, 'but I'd like to ask just two more questions.'

'All right, go ahead,' he said.

I said: 'When you were negotiating that lease, you were in my bachelor apartment. You walked over to the bookcase and pulled back a set of dummy books to expose a hi-fi. How did you know it was there?'

'Heavens,' she said, 'I've seen thousands of hi-fi's concealed behind dummy sets of books.'

'Answer the question. How did you know it was there? Had you ever been in that apartment before? Remember you're under oath. Your answer can be checked.'

She hesitated, then said: 'I had been in the apartment before.'

'You had lived there?'

'Yes.'

'Before I moved in?'

'Yes.'

'You vacated the apartment so I could move in?'

'All right, I did. I moved my things out so you could move in.'

I said to Helen Hart: 'May I have that sketch, please? The last one, the one that you said bore a startling resemblance to the man you saw peering in the window.'

She handed me the sketch.

I said to Helen Hart: 'That's a sketch of the man you saw peering in the window?'

'That's a sketch of the man I saw peering in the window when I emerged from the shower,' she said positively.

I thrust the sketch in front of Bernice Clinton and said: 'Do you recognize that man – yes or no?'

She looked at the sketch, then she looked at me, then she looked at Helen Hart. She took a deep breath. She said: 'There's something about the face that's . . . that's vaguely familiar, but I couldn't recognize the man from the sketch.'

I turned to Moxey Malone. 'Did you get that real estate folder?'

'Yes,' he said.

'May I have it, please?'

He handed it to me.

I turned it over and thrust the picture of Montrose Levining Carson in front of Bernice Clinton. I said: 'Do you know this man? Answer yes or no.'

She looked at the picture, hesitated a moment ,then said: 'Yes. I know him.'

I said: 'Is he the man who is paying the rent on the apartment in Santa Ana that you are occupying under the same of Agnes Dayton?'

'Oh, come,' Fillmore said. 'We've decided we aren't going into a question of morals here.'

I said: 'It isn't a question of morals. Take a look at his picture, then take a look at this sketch that Miss Hart has identified. Then let me ask this witness whether it isn't a fact that she wasn't employed by Herbert Jason Dowling at all, but the whole thing was engineered by Montrose L. Carson in an attempt to make me believe I was dealing with Dowling.

'Then let me point out to her that this is a murder rap and she's in it. That she's already committed perjury and that she can go to the gas-chamber in California as an accessory unless she wants to change her testimony right now.'

Abruptly Bernice Clinton straightened in the witness-chair and said: 'All right, I'm not going to be the goat in this thing. There *wasn't* any prowler.'

Fillmore leaned forward. 'No prowler?' he asked.

'No prowler,' she said.

'I think perhaps you'd better explain,' Fillmore said.

Bernice said: 'I'm going to tell this story, but I'm going to tell it in my own way. Mr Carson wanted me to go to the Swim and Tan Motel and at a certain prearranged time I was to call the police and tell them that there was a Peeping Tom looking in the window.'

'And there wasn't any Peeping Tom?' I asked.

'Not that I could see.'

'You had the shade up?' Fillmore asked.

'I had the shade up and my outer clothes off. I was down to a bra and panties, and I called the police. Then I threw a robe over me and was like that when the police came. I reported the prowler, and the description I gave the police was a general description that would

182

fit almost anyone. Mr Carson told me to make the description ambiguous and general so I could change it and identify someone later on if I had to.'

'But what was the idea of all this?' Fillmore asked.

'Mr Carson wanted to get control of Dowling's corporation. He had a tip that Dowling was having a surreptitious affair with a young woman named Irene Addis and that their meeting-place was the Swim and Tan Motel. Mr Carson wanted to verify that information before he took any definite action.

'He had a tip there was to be a meeting there the night Helen Hart saw the prowler. It was a false tip, but while he was looking in the window of the unit he thought Dowling was occupying, Helen Hart stepped out of the shower. The light was shining on Mr Carson's face. He was afraid she'd be able to give police a description of him that might make trouble, so he got me to go to the same motel on a night when he had a perfect alibi and report that I had seen the prowler. I was to give a general description that would fit almost anyone.'

There was a period of silence while the people were digesting this information.

'But Carson gave Irene Addis a job in his office, didn't he?' I asked.

'Of course he did.'

'Why did he do that?'

'So he'd have a good excuse to hire a detective agency to check up on her and turn up her affair with Dowling. That's why he hired you people, but you were too dumb to find the connection. That's why I had to send you a wire, giving you a tip.'

'How do you know all this?' Fillmore asked.

'Because Carson told me.'

'And why did he tell *you* all this?' Fillmore asked.

She met his eyes. 'Because I was Dowling's mistress, and Carson tried to use me by telling me a lot of lies about Herbert Dowling. I know now they were lies and I know Herbert was levelling with me. I'm finished with Montrose Carson and all his chicanery. I don't have to put up with his kind any more. Now I can be a lady. Herbert Dowling always told me he would provide for me, and he was a man of his word.'

Fillmore asked: 'How did it happen that you identified Donald Lam as the prowler?'

'I was acting under Mr Carson's instructions. Now I realize just how he tried to use me; the lies he told. I'm finished.'

Fillmore settled back in his chair and looked at Sellers. Sellers was sitting completely dumbfounded, trying to adjust his mind to this new twist in the case.

I said: 'And you were told by Mr Carson to negotiate with me for the corner lot?'

'Yes.'

'And you had no actual contact with Dowling?'

She started to answer, hesitated, then finally said: 'About that particular lot, no. I was intimate with Herbert Dowling and I'm proud to have been his mistress. My only regret is that I permitted others to plant the seeds of suspicion in my mind so that I was turned against Herbert Dowling there at the last. I would give anything to be able to undo the wrong that I did a very noble and a very honourable gentleman.'

Fillmore said: 'You *were* Dowling's mistress?'

'How often must I tell you? I was his mistress.'

'And what were you to Carson?'

'I was nothing but his tool; his blind, credulous tool.

184

He played on my jealousy. He told me Herbert Dowling had another woman.'

'And Carson paid for the apartment in Santa Ana?' I asked.

'Carson paid for the apartment in Santa Ana,' she flared. 'He wanted a place where he could contact me without anyone knowing. That apartment was for his business, not for love-making. . . . I realize, now that it is too late, what a blind, utterly naïve, credulous fool I was.'

· 'Did Carson tell you anything about the murder of Dowling?' I asked.

'Certainly not! He asked me to do certain things. I did them.'

Fillmore turned to Sellers. 'What are *you* going to do now?' he asked.

Sellers looked at me. 'I think Lam has some explaining to do.'

I shook my head. 'I'm going to waive extradition now. I'm going back to California with Sergeant Sellers.'

'You're *what*?' Fillmore asked incredulously.

'I'm waiving extradition,' I said. 'I'm going back to California in the custody of Sergeant Sellers. I'm going voluntarily. Sellers is a square cop. When he thinks he's right, he's tough. He hates crooks. He hates double-crossers. There are times when he doesn't like me. But he's a square shooter. I'm going back with him.'

Fillmore frowned.

Moxey Malone got to his feet, started to say something, then paused as Helen Hart tugged at the edge of his coat. She gently pulled him back down into the seat.

'I guess that's all there is on this hearing,' Fillmore

said. 'If Lam wants to waive extradition, there's nothing for me to pass on. The hearing is adjourned.'

Fillmore got up and left the room.

Moxey Malone came over to me and said: 'Look, Lam, do you know what you're doing?'

'I know what I'm doing.'

Sellers said: 'Okay, Wise Guy. Thanks for the boost, and you *may* be right. If you master-minded this thing so you know the answer, I want to know it. I don't want to be used. You get me, Lam? I don't want to be used.'

'Nobody's using you,' I told him. 'I'm waiving extradition and going back. Now where does that leave you?'

'It leaves me,' he said, 'getting on the first available plane before you have a chance to change that foxy mind of yours.'

'I'll do better than that,' Sergeant Ransom said, looking at his watch. 'There's a plane to Los Angeles via Palm Springs in half an hour. I'll get you there.'

Helen Hart came forward. 'Donald,' she said, 'I have an idea you know what you're doing, but . . . if you need anything – anything at all – Mr Malone and I are ready to help.'

'Thanks,' I told her. 'I don't think I'll need anything. Sellers is honest. At times he's a little stubborn.'

'At times I'm awfully damn stubborn,' Sellers said.

'I think you're a brute!' she flared at him. 'You had no business smashing that boy's jaw with your fist.'

'Okay, lady, okay,' Sellers said. 'I was impulsive. I was mad.'

She said: 'I hope some day some big bruiser gets mad at you and lets you see how it feels.'

Sellers grinned and said: 'I know how it feels. I've stopped lots of them. Come on, Lam.'

I held out my hand to Helen Hart. 'Thanks,' I said.

She took my hand in both of hers. 'Let me know how things come out, Donald.'

'I'll let you know,' I said. 'Bye now, and thanks for the buggy ride.'

Ransom said: 'If we're going to get in a car, get out to the airport and get on that plane, we'd better get going.'

'We're getting going,' Sellers said. 'Come on, Lam.'

Chapter 17

As we strapped our seat belts into place, Sellers said:
'Now look, Lam, I'm not buying any of your theories
sight unseen. I'm not buying *anything*.'

'Don't buy, then,' I said.

The pilot started the motors. The plane taxied on
down to take-off position and then waited while the pilot
revved up the motors in turn, tested the controls.

Sellers said: 'What do *you* think happened?'

'I'm afraid I'd be trying to sell you something,' I said.
'You wouldn't like that.'

The pilot gunned the plane into motion and we went
down the ramp, then zoomed up into the air. The plane
levelled off into an easier climb, the illuminated sign
about the seat belts went dark.

Sellers said: 'You don't need to be so damned cagey
about things. I'm sorry about that sock on the jaw, Lam.
I was mad.'

'You had no business getting mad.'

'I know it, Lam. A good cop doesn't let his feelings get
the best of him that way. I'm sorry. I told you I was
sorry. I apologize. Damn it, if you want to be mean
about it, I'll stand still and let you sock me one.'

'Okay,' I said. 'You're sorry.'

'All right, Pint Size. Now what's the pitch?'

I said: 'There can only be one pitch, but I wouldn't try to sell *you*.'

'All right, I'll give up. Try and sell me. I'm not going to buy, but try and sell me. It will keep you in practice.'

'I'm not trying to sell you anything. Go ahead, get me back to Los Angeles. Newspaper reporters will meet the plane. You can tell them you've caught the murderer. Then Helen Hart will identify Carson as the Peeping Tom, Bernice Clinton will confess to perjury, and somebody's face will be red. It won't be mine.'

Sellers thought that over while the plane gained altitude.

'Keep talking,' he said after a while.

'There's no reason why I should,' I told him. 'I'm getting even with you for a sock on the puss. You hurt me. Now then, you can take your medicine. You're going back to Los Angeles. Helen Hart and her attorney, Moxey Malone, will see that the press is alerted. The Phœnix reporters will find out about the extradition hearing in Fillmore's office. They'll sell the story to the wire services. The Los Angeles papers will pick it up and play it big. By the time we get there you'll have an audience. They'll ask questions. It'll be interesting to hear your answers. This is your egg. You've laid it. Now hatch it. I'll watch. I'll be right there. I'll be handcuffed to you. You can't get rid of me until you've booked me.'

'Now look, Lam. I apologized for that sock on the jaw.'

'It still hurts.'

'What the hell do you want me to do?' he blazed. 'Kiss it and make it all well for Mother's little manikin?'

'No,' I said. 'I just want to have the satisfaction of seeing you put on the carpet at a press interview with reporters. They'll have photographers and press cameras with flash-bulbs and you'll make a statement. Then when you get all done, I'll make a statement.'

'The hell you will!' he said. 'You'll have nothing to say.'

'In that event,' I said, 'the press will sense a big story and the fact that you cut it off.

'The reporters won't like that. Some of them will write paragraphs to the effect that Sergeant Frank Sellers, who is himself under arrest in Phœnix for brutality and is now out on a two-thousand-dollar bail, kept the prisoner from making any statement. Moxey Malone, a prominent Phœnix attorney, announced that not only is Sellers to be prosecuted for aggravated assault, smashing the prisoner's head against the wall of an apartment, but Malone has been retained as an attorney to file a civil suit asking for fifty thousand dollars' damages. . . . Oh, well, play it your own way.'

I settled down in the seat, yawned and closed my eyes.

'You sonofabitch,' Sellers said, 'you go to sleep on me and I'll give you the works.'

I said: 'You as much as lay a finger on me, and Moxey Malone will have your badge.'

'Now look, Donald, this isn't getting us anywhere.'

'It's getting us to Los Angeles,' I said, 'and that's where I want to be. You didn't want me to sell you anything because you didn't want to buy it and –'

'If it sounds good I *might* buy it at that,' Sellers said.

'No,' I told him, 'you'd louse it up somewhere. You get me on back to Los Angeles. I'll get an attorney, I'll talk with him and pass instructions along. Then the firm of Cool and Lam will solve the murder while you're crucifying yourself with a statement to the reporters.'

'I don't have to make any comment to the reporters,' Sellers said.

I laughed at that one.

'What's funny about it?'

'Remember that they'll have had the whole story of the hearing in Fillmore's office relayed to them by the wire services. They'll be out to elaborate on that story.'

I closed my eyes again.

Sellers said: 'I don't have to take you to Los Angeles.'

'I've waived extradition. I'm under arrest,' I said.

'I can do it my way,' Sellers said. 'I believe you have a rented car at Palm Springs?'

'Sure,' I said. 'I'll tell Bertha to go get it.'

I sucked in a deep yawn, settled back in the chair and closed my eyes.

I could feel Sellers trying to think things out. Once I half raised my lids and surreptitiously studied him from the corner of my eyes.

Sellers was frowning. His lips were moving silently as he tried to formulate soundless words in which to clothe his thoughts.

After a while the stewardess announced that we were approaching Palm Springs and should fasten seat belts again. Sellers nudged me with an ungentle elbow. 'Okay, Pint Size, wake up.'

'What's the matter?' I asked, feigning drowsiness.

'You aren't going to get to talk with those Los Angeles reporters.'

'Why not?'

'You're getting off at Palm Springs.'

'That won't do you any good,' I said. 'When the plane gets in to Los Angeles and you aren't aboard, the reporters will talk with the stewardess and find out where you got off. Then they'll really be laying for you.'

'Let them lay,' Sellers said. 'Come on, you're getting off.'

We got off at Palm Springs.

'You got a car here,' Sellers said. 'It's a rented car. Where is it?'

'At the airport.'

'Where did you leave the keys?'

'Underneath the rubber mat on the floor-board.'

Sellers had me point out the car, dug out the keys and fitted the key in the ignition lock.

'Where are we going now?' I asked.

'We're going to headquarters my way,' Sellers said.

'This heap is costing me ten cents a mile,' I said.

'Ain't that too bad,' Sellers commented. 'You don't co-operate with me and I don't co-operate with you, see?'

'Now look,' I told him. 'I've got some rights. I want to be taken before the nearest and most accessible magistrate.'

'You're talking to my deaf ear. I can't hear you.'

'Okay,' I said, 'have it your way. By the time Moxey Malone gets done with you, you'll have a hearing aid for that ear.'

'Now look,' Sellers said, 'this Moxey Malone – there's a guy that's not at all co-operative.'

'He co-operates with me all right.'

'What would you say if I turned you loose, just turned you right free, spanking loose?'

'You can't do it,' I told him. 'You're an officer of the law. I'm in your custody.'

'I could let you escape.'

'I wouldn't escape.'

'All right, what the hell *do* you want?'

'I want to get turned loose,' I said. 'I want to get my good name vindicated. Then Bertha Cool and I are going to solve this murder and this time we're not going to let any cop take the credit for it. We're going to be the ones who get the credit for solving it.'

I could see the muscles of Sellers's jaw bulge as he clamped his teeth together.

After a while he fished a cigar from his pocket, pushed it into his face and started chewing on it without lighting up.

We were headed over the mountains on the Palms to Pines Highway. Sellers probably felt they'd be less apt to look for him on that road in case someone tried to catch him and get a story.

'You can't solve anything,' he said, 'any more than it's solved already. I know who killed Dowling.'

'Do you?' I asked. 'And I'd like to know how you are going to prove it.'

'Bernice Clinton will crack up,' he said.

'Bernice is an accomplice,' I told him. 'You can't convict Carson on the uncorroborated evidence of an accomplice.'

'We've got the gun.'

'Sure,' I said, 'you've got the gun. You used that as evidence against me. Now you want to use it as evidence against Carson. How do you know Bernice Clinton didn't plant it when *she* was in the apartment?'

The thought hit Sellers between the eyes. 'What the hell!' he said.

'I'm not saying anything,' I told him. 'This time Bertha and I are going to solve the case.'

'You can't get any evidence the police can't get,' Sellers said.

'That's right,' I told him, 'I can't get any evidence the police can't get. But the police won't be looking in the right place. I'll look in the right place and look there first.'

'Now look, Lam, give me a break on this thing. You know damn well it isn't going to do any good for you to solve a murder case. You aren't paid for that. You're just a private investigator. What's more, Bertha won't ride along with it. She'll give me the breaks.'

'Not after she hears about you socking me on the chin,' I said.

'Oh, forget that!'

'I can't. It still hurts.'

'You could have got hurt a lot worse than that. I'll tell you something, you pint-sized bastard, you aren't solving any murder case. If you don't kick through, by God I'll just keep this damn car driving around southern California at ten cents a mile until the damn case solves itself. By that time you'll have a bill for mileage that will have Bertha tearing her hair.'

'It's okay,' I said. 'I'll collect it in civil damages by the time Moxey Malone gets done with you in Phoenix.'

'You can't collect from me,' Sellers said. 'I'm a cop. I don't have anything except my salary.'

'You got an equity in a car,' I said. 'We could use that.'

'Damn you,' Sellers said, 'would you make a personal matter out of it?'

'It was your personal fist that socked me.'

'Okay, okay,' Sellers said, 'all right. I give in, Pint Size. Now come on, kick through.'

'Would you follow up a lead if I gave it to you?'

'What kind of a lead?'

'A lead that would solve the murder.'

'Okay, okay, what do you want?'

I said: 'We stop at the first phone. We telephone Bertha Cool to meet us in Santa Ana. Then we go to the Corinthian Arms and we search that apartment Bernice Clinton had under the name of Agnes Dayton. If there's any incriminating evidence, any letters or anything of that sort, we'll find them there.'

'There won't be anything,' Sellers said.

'Okay,' I told him, 'play it your way if you want to be dumb.'

There was a service station a mile ahead. Sellers thought things over for that mile. Abruptly he swung into the service station and showed his badge. 'I want to use your phone,' he said. 'It's official business.'

Ten minutes later he was back in the car. 'Okay,' he said, 'Bertha's meeting us. We don't have any search warrant.'

I said: 'You have reasonable grounds after what she said in Phoenix. If you haven't wasted too much time already, we can still get there in time.'

'We got all the time in the world,' Sellers said.

'Not with that babe, you haven't,' I told him.

Sellers pushed down the throttle on the car. 'Okay, Wise Guy,' he said, 'I'm going to buy it. I swore I'd never buy another one of your stories, but I'm going to buy this one. Hang on because we're going to travel.'

Chapter 18

Bertha Cool was waiting for us in front of the Corinthian Arms in Santa Ana.

As we drove up, Bertha got out of her car and came striding down the sidewalk. She looked past Sellers, said to me: 'Now what the hell have you been doing? You –'

'Hold it, Bertha,' Sellers said, 'the guy may be on the up and up.'

'What!' Bertha exclaimed.

'You heard me,' Sellers said. 'It isn't as simple a case as it appeared.'

Bertha said: 'You told me you had him dead to rights.'

'I thought I did,' Sellers said. 'There were some things about the case I didn't know.'

Bertha glowered at me, then said to Sellers: 'Well, it would help a lot if you'd make up your mind.'

'It would help me a lot if I could make it up,' Sellers said. 'Right now I'm just riding along. I've got a bear by the tail and can't let go.'

'What are we doing here?'

'We're going to look in someone's apartment.'

Bertha said to me: 'These unorthodox methods of yours. My God, I even start on a cut-and-dried case for a commercial report on a business leak and you get all tied up in murder!'

196

She strode towards the entrance of the apartment house, following Sellers. I brought up the rear.

Sellers found the manager and explained that he'd like to take a look in the Agnes Dayton apartment.

The manager called a lawyer and told Sellers nothing doing, unless he had a warrant.

Sellers stewed and fumed. He got the chief of the Santa Ana police on the phone. The police chief called the city attorney and the district attorney.

While they were having a hassle, a taxicab drove up in front of the building and Bernice Clinton got out.

The manager said: 'Here's Miss Dayton now.'

Bernice took a look at the gathering and said: 'What's this all about?'

'We want to take a look in your apartment,' Sellers said.

'You got a warrant?' she asked.

'That's exactly the point I raised,' the manager said.

'Thank you,' Bernice said to the manager, breezed on past us, went into the elevator and went up.

Sellers was controlling himself with an effort. He thought things over, then turned and strode back to the sidewalk.

At the car he turned on me. 'Okay, Pint Size,' he said, 'you master-minded me into one hell of a situation. Now the Santa Ana papers will be full of it.'

'Why don't you go ahead and search the apartment?'

'I don't dare to after all those legal rulings.'

'Why don't you get a warrant?'

'I don't have evidence enough.'

I said: 'Okay, handle it your way.'

'You don't know what's happened with all these damn court decisions lately,' Sellers said. 'They've taken the handcuffs off the crooks and put them on the wrists of the officers.'

'All right,' I told him. 'You're running the show, I'm not.'

'Oh, I thought you were. You were making the suggestions.'

'You didn't adopt my suggestions.'

'I tried to follow through. I was giving you a break.'

Bertha Cool said: 'It's a hell of a note when the law can't search a person's apartment.'

'He can,' I said to Bertha.

'What do you mean, he can?'

'Sure I can,' Sellers said, 'if I want to stick my neck out getting a warrant.'

I said to Bertha, as though explaining a problem to a ten-year-old child and completely ignoring Sellers: 'This girl admitted perjury in Phoenix. They probably arrested her and she arranged to put up bail. The bail was furnished by someone who had to have her out of the jurisdiction of the law. She admitted lying in connection with a murder case. She admitted being an accessory before the fact. All Sellers has to do is to go up there and arrest her on suspicion of murder. Once he's arrested her, he gets in the apartment. Once he gets in the apartment, he can look around, can't he? He's got reasonable grounds for everything.'

Sellers said: 'By George, I *can* do that! I can take her into custody as a suspect in that murder.'

'Not without releasing me,' I said. 'You can't have two suspects.'

Sellers thought that over.

'And,' I said to Bertha, 'if Sellers really wanted to be smart, he could admit his defeat, drive off, go around the block and sit where he can keep an eye on the apartment.

'This girl was in big trouble in Phoenix. She got out of it. That took money. She got an aeroplane to fly her direct to Santa Ana. That's the only way she could have got everything squared up and got here this soon. That took money. Inside of fifteen or twenty minutes she'll come out of the apartment and walk across the street to that mailbox to mail a letter. That will give her a chance to see if the coast is clear. If she thinks the coast is clear, inside of five minutes a taxicab will drive up to the door. This babe will come out of the apartment hell-for-leather and tell the cab-driver either to take her to the airport or to someplace where Montrose L. Carson is waiting.'

'Why Carson?' Bertha asked.

'He's the only one left who could have put up the money to get her out of Phoenix,' I said.

Bertha looked at me, blinking her eyes. 'Fry me for an oyster,' she said.

I yawned. 'However, Sellers is playing it cautiously. He doesn't want to take a chance. So I guess he'll keep me under arrest, take me back to Los Angeles, and then I'll talk to newspaper reporters.

'The reporters will have quite a time. They've got the story of the hearing in Phoenix by this time, and after I talk with them they'll have the story of this apartment fiasco in Santa Ana.'

'You're the one who talked me into coming here,' Sellers said.

I yawned again.

Sellers climbed into my rented car and said: 'You'd better get in, Bertha.'

'Where are you going?'

'I'm going to take him to headquarters in Los Angeles.'

'Then I'll drive my car,' Bertha said.

'Leave it parked there,' Sellers told her. 'Get in here.'

Bertha got in the back seat.

Sellers drove away, circled two blocks, came back and parked down the street where he could keep an eye on the mailbox.

We had been there about five minutes when Bernice Clinton came out of the apartment carrying a letter so ostentatiously that we could see it a block and a half away.

She mailed the letter, looked casually up and down the street, returned to the apartment.

Sellers was out of the car like a shot as soon as she had re-entered the apartment house. He entered a drugstore which had a phone booth, went into the phone booth, dropped a dime and started dialling.

Bertha Cool said to me: 'You've raised hell. You've got the agency into more trouble than it can ever get out of. You've lost your licence and maybe mine. You've antagonized Frank Sellers. You've –'

'Shut up,' I said.

'What the hell do you mean, telling me to shut up!' Bertha screamed.

'You heard me,' I told her. 'You're going to have to eat all those words and you can make the dish smaller by using fewer words.'

'Why, you . . . you . . .'

Bertha sputtered into apoplectic silence.

A taxi came up to the Corinthian Arms. Bernice Clinton must have been waiting just inside the door, because the taxi had no sooner stopped and the driver got out than the door opened and Bernice came out, carrying a suitcase and a brief-case. The cab-driver put the baggage in the cab, waited until Bernice had got in the cab and closed the door. Then he walked around, got into the driver's side and the cab drove away.

I could see Bernice turning around looking through the rear window to see if anyone was following.

'What the hell!' Bertha said. 'What's that damn, dumb cop doing telephoning while she's making her getaway?'

I said: 'He's running his business. Let's concentrate on ours for a change and worry about us instead of Frank Sellers.'

'Well, you've given us plenty to worry about,' Bertha said. 'I'll say that for you.'

Bertha tried to catch Sellers's eye and signal him. He kept his back to us. Finally he turned and looked up.

Bertha made frantic signs, pointing down the street.

Sellers might not have seen her. He turned back into the telephone booth and did some more phoning.

After a while Sellers came sauntering out and leisurely got in the car.

Bertha was so mad she was sputtering. 'My God Almighty,' she said, 'what a jerk you turned out to be! Donald, here, told you exactly what was going to happen, and you had to go in there and start telephoning for advice while she made her getaway. Didn't you see my signals?'

'Sure I saw them,' Sellers said.

'Well,' Bertha said, 'for your information, if it will give you any satisfaction, your bird has flown the coop.'

Sellers said: 'If it will give you any satisfaction, the bird has flown right into the coop.'

'What do you mean?' Bertha said.

'I'll explain later,' Sellers said.

Bertha's face got purple. I said: 'Take it easy, Bertha. Sellers simply phoned the Santa Ana Police Department. They phoned the taxicab dispatcher and said: "You just sent a cab to the Corinthian Arms Apartments. We want to know where the fare goes." You see, they have a radio dispatcher system, and the cab will report in as soon as the fare gives an address, stating where it's bound for, whether it's the airport or someplace else.'

'Fry me for an oyster!' Bertha said.

Sellers looked me over. 'Wise guy!'

I yawned.

Sellers pulled a fresh cigar out of his pocket, clamped it in between his lips and started chewing on it. After a while he got out of the car, walked into the telephone booth again, dialled a number, came back, got in the car and started the motor.

'Where?' I asked him.

'You're so smart, dope it out,' Sellers said.

'I will,' I told him. 'It's the nearest airport where private planes can land.'

'Don't you think that'd be a little obvious?' Sellers asked.

'It might be but it's the fastest.'

'But not the best,' Sellers said, grinning.

'Where to?' I asked.

'You'll find out,' Sellers said.

I settled back in the cushions, and Sellers drove through Santa Ana down towards Newport Beach.

'Has he gone nuts?' Bertha said.

'It makes sense,' I told her. 'Carson's meeting her at Newport in a private yacht. She'll get aboard, they'll announce they're sailing for Catalina and wind up in

Ensenada – just a nice little week-end yachting party that is too common to attract attention. They'll get married and then neither one can testify against the other. Bernice used her head, and now the guy's going to have to marry her.'

'I ought to go back and get my car,' Bertha said. 'They'll fine me for parking over the time limit.'

'You stay right here with us,' Sellers told her.

'For your information,' I told Bertha, 'I've rented this car, and Sellers has taken it over. We're paying ten cents a mile.'

Bertha came up with such violence I thought she was going to wreck the springs on the rear seat.

'What!' she yelled.

'Ten cents a mile,' I told her.

'Why, you – What the hell right have *you* got to confiscate Donald's car? Who the hell do you think you are?' Bertha screamed at Sellers.

Sellers, watching a traffic signal ahead, shifted the cigar in his mouth and didn't even turn his head.

Bertha kept it up for half a mile, then subsided into silence; a futile, tooth-gnashing silence of utter frustration.

Sellers didn't seem to be in any hurry. We drove in a leisurely manner to Newport, then to the swank yacht club. Sellers flashed his badge and his I.D. card, went in and parked the car.

A police officer was waiting for him. 'This way,' he said.

'You two come along and keep quiet,' Sellers said.

We walked down to a private landing. A big, ocean-going, twin-screw Diesel yacht was tied up. A police officer was on guard at the gangplank.

The officer passed us through. We went down to a cabin.

Montrose L. Carson, Bernice Clinton and a couple of officers were sitting around a table.

Carson's face was a mask of frozen rage.

'I presume *you're* responsible for this,' he said, as I walked in.

I bowed.

Sellers said: '*I'll* do the talking. *I'm* responsible for it, Carson.'

'I'll have your licence,' Carson said to me. 'You've double-crossed me. You have taken both sides of a case. You –'

'Shut up,' Sellers said. 'You hired these people to find a leak in your business. There wasn't any leak. That was all a fabrication on your part for the purpose of getting these people to pull some chestnuts out of the fire for you. You didn't hire them to solve a murder, and you didn't hire them to commit one.'

'How do I know what he did?' Carson asked. 'I wouldn't put anything past him.'

Sellers turned to the officer. 'Have you searched him?'

The officer nodded. 'Didn't get anything out of him.'

'What about the broad?' Sellers asked.

Bernice Clinton said: 'I am not a broad, I have not been searched, I am not going to be searched. My baggage is not going to be touched. I am a woman, I am not going to have a lot of men pawing me over and getting a lot of cheap satisfaction, claiming that they're performing their official duties. I demand a matron. I –'

Sellers jerked his thumb at Bertha Cool. 'Deputize her,' he said to the officer.

The officer grinned and said: 'What's her name?'

'Bertha Cool.'

The officer said: 'Bertha Cool, in the name of the law I deputize you to assist as a citizen, I appoint you as a matron and instruct you to search this prisoner.'

Bernice Clinton got white. She got to her feet and said: 'How dare you! How dare you! You can't touch me! You can't –'

'Am I deputized?' Bertha Cool asked.

'You're deputized,' the officer said.

'Where's a private room?' Bertha asked.

The officer nodded towards a door. 'That's a state-room.'

Bertha said: 'Come on, dearie.'

'You go to hell,' Bernice Clinton said.

Bertha moved over, and Bernice came towards her, clawing, and screaming epithets.

Bertha upended her, wrapped an arm around her waist and carried her through the door as though Bernice had been a sack of groceries.

A third officer came in, and Carson was escorted to the pier.

Sellers sat down and grinned.

The officer grinned back.

Sellers jerked a thumb at me and said: 'Sit down, Pint Size.'

We heard sound from behind the door; a banging and the sound of a voice raised in shrill vilification. The yacht jarred as though the hull was hitting against something solid. The wall bulged under an impact.

After about ten minutes Bertha came out with Bernice Clinton in tow.

Bernice looked as though she had been through a meat

grinder. Her hair was in strings. Her skirt was torn. There was a hole in her blouse.

'I searched her,' Bertha said.

'What did you find?'

Bertha tossed a document on the table. 'This was folded and inside her bra,' she said.

The officers pounced on it.

I didn't get a chance to see it, but after a while Sellers nodded and said: 'That does it. That furnishes motivation. That's a will by Herbert Jason Dowling, leaving everything he has in the world to Bernice Clinton.'

'When was it executed?' I asked.

'Two years ago,' Sellers said.

I said: 'It isn't worth the paper it's written on. Dowling left a son. He also left a wife by a common-law marriage. He and this woman had registered as man and wife in states where common-law marriage is binding. He had a child by her. He can't leave his property to somebody else without disinheriting them specifically, and I think some of his property was community property.'

Bernice Clinton said: 'You cheap little squirt! You don't know as much as you think you do. Take another look at that will. It was drawn by a lawyer who knows his way around. It provides that if any person claimed to be an heir, a spouse or any relation, that such person was to be given one dollar.'

I said: 'You couldn't inherit in any case. They'll pin a murder rap on you. A murderer can't inherit the victim's property.'

Sellers said: 'This will is what we want – this and evidence of attempted flight.'

'What are you going to do now?' the officer asked.

'Book them for suspicion of murder,' Sellers said.

'You're not going to make a case!' Bernice Clinton shouted. 'I've had enough of your interference, you cheap, tin-star, gum-shoe, stool-pigeon sons-of-bitches! You –'

Bertha swung with her arm, grabbed Bernice's torn blouse, twisted it tight.

'Shut up,' Bertha said, 'you're talking about my brother officers.'

Bernice had had enough of Bertha. She shut up.

The officers grinned at each other.

Sellers walked over to me. 'Beat it, 'he said.

'I'm released?'

'You're free as the air,' he said. 'You're a private citizen. Nobody has anything on you. On your way.'

I said: 'You can't do it. You're an officer of the law. You were instructed to put me under arrest.'

'And I was instructed over long-distance telephone to turn you loose if this panned out,' Sellers said. 'What the hell did you think I was doing in there on the telephone, in addition to getting a line on the destination of this taxicab?'

'What about Bertha?' I asked.

Sellers grinned and said: 'We need a good strong matron to subdue the prisoner. Otherwise this broad would claim we attacked her and tried to molest her sexually while we were taking her to jail. Bertha's deputized.'

'Do I get wages?' Bertha asked.

'You get wages,' Sellers said, 'such as they are. You have to make a claim against the county.'

'Don't worry, I'll make the claim,' Bertha said.

Bernice Clinton was scrambling to her feet. She started

to say something, then caught Bertha's eye and subsided into silence.

'We'll search the yacht for additional evidence,' Sellers said. 'You can search the baggage of the female prisoner, Mrs Cool, and we'll be on our way.'

Her turned to me and jerked his thumb towards the door. 'Get going, Pint Size.'

I got going.

Chapter 19

The office of Herbert Jason Dowling was closed on account of his death. I found Doris Gilman, the girl who had been dining with him in the cafeteria, in her apartment.

'You're the man who followed me up in the elevator and down the corridor to the office,' she said when I had introduced myself.

'That's right,' I told her. 'What's more, I followed you from the cafeteria where you and Mr Dowling had your surreptitious lunch.'

Her eyes met mine. She studied me for a moment in thoughtful speculation, then said: 'All right, what do you want?'

'I want the truth and it had better be the truth because you're mixed up in a murder case.'

'What do you want to know?'

I said: 'Why were you meeting so surreptitiously?'

'On account of Bernice Clinton.'

'Did you know she was watching you in the cafeteria?'

'What!' Doris Gilman exclaimed. 'She was watching?'

I nodded.

'That explains it then,' she said.

'Explains what?'

'The murder.'

'How come?'

'Bernice is . . . dangerous,' she said.

'She's had her fangs pulled,' I said. 'Were you making any time with Dowling? What were you after? Marriage, money or –'

'I wasn't making any time with him,' she said, 'and the situation wasn't what you think.'

'In this business I've heard that statement so many times I get tired of it.'

She said: 'Dowling paid no more attention to me as a woman than he would have paid to a sack of potatoes.'

'That wasn't the way I saw it,' I said. 'You were using your eyes and –'

'Sure I was using my eyes,' she said. 'He wanted something I couldn't give him. He wanted something he could never get. Therefore, why shouldn't I look for the side of the bread that had the butter?'

'What did he want?' I asked. 'You?'

'Don't be silly! He could have had me on a silver platter any time he crooked his finger. He wanted Irene Addis.'

'Oh-oh,' I said.

'And he came to me because he thought I could engineer the deal to get her back.'

'And you knew you couldn't?'

'I knew I couldn't and I wanted him to see that I was available.'

'You approached Irene?'

'I did not. I knew how she felt. I strung the situation along, hoping it would work out. It might have at that, only – If Bernice saw us – He was deathly afraid of Bernice. She said she'd kill him rather than let him go.'

'She didn't have any legal hold. Why didn't he tell her to go roll her hoop?'

'She had plenty of hold. While he was infatuated with her she was putting feathers on her nest.'

'Letters?' I asked.

'Letters, tape-recordings, photographs . . . she had everything.'

'What did she want?'

'Marriage.'

'Would she have accepted a property settlement?'

'Not at the last. He'd put it off too long. When he could have bought her off he didn't, and then she became fantastic in her demands. She wanted to be Mrs Dowling. She wanted social position, recognition – she's gone completely crazy on that. She wants to be "recognized". She wants to be Mrs Somebody Important.'

'She was starting to put butter on both sides of the bread,' I said. 'Or perhaps I should say she was buttering two slices of bread at the same time.'

'Such as what?'

I said: 'Montrose L. Carson wanted to work from the inside and take over the Dowling company, tossing Dowling out on his ear. He was within an ace of doing it. He could have done it if some good juicy scandal had rocked the company right at this critical time, and Carson was getting ready to furnish the scandal.'

'Carson!' she exclaimed. 'Then *that's* why he got Irene Addis working with him.'

'Sure,' I said, 'he was setting a trap for her. The whole thing was a trap. Bernice had swapped horses in the middle of the stream and made a pretty good trade at that. I don't know whether Carson had promised to marry her and give her the social position and respectability she craved, but he had at least made *some* commitments. He was maintaining her in a really high-class apartment in Santa Ana under the name of Agnes Dayton.'

Doris looked at me with big eyes.

'And,' I said, 'Bernice Clinton has a will executed by Dowling and delivered to her for safekeeping and –'

'Oh, that!' she said. 'That doesn't mean anything.'

'How do you know it doesn't?' I asked.

'Because Dowling made a later will, entirely in his own handwriting, leaving everything to Irene Addis and to her son. He told me he was going to deliver that will to Irene and tell her that if he couldn't get free from Bernice's clutches he at least wanted her to know –'

'Wait a minute,' I interrupted, 'he told you he was going to *deliver* that will to Irene?'

'Yes. He asked me if I thought it would make any difference in her attitude towards him.'

'He was going to *deliver* it to Irene?'

'Yes. That's what I said.'

'Then he must have taken it with him to the Swim and Tan Motel – but it wasn't on his body after the murder.'

'That's right,' she said. 'He put his cards on the table with me there at the cafeteria. He told me he was meeting Irene that night but he didn't say where. He asked me what to do about the will.'

'And you told him to tell her about it and deliver it to her?'

'That's right. By that time I saw he was all wrapped up in Irene and as far as he was concerned there would never be another woman in the world.'

'You knew about Irene's son?'

'Yes.'

'Did he ever acknowledge to you that he was the father?'

'Yes.'

'And you told him to take the will and show it to Irene?'

'Not only show it to her but deliver it to her for safe-keeping. . . . Tell me, Donald, what would happen if the person who killed him took that will and destroyed it?'

'That depends,' I said, 'on whether we could prove the existence of the will. But we'd have to prove by indisputable evidence that the will existed, what its terms were, and that he hadn't changed his mind and destroyed it voluntarily before he went to the motel. That's a pretty big order. . . . Now, getting back to Irene's son. He acknowledged to you that he was the father?'

'Yes. I told you that.'

'Do you have any correspondence with him? Did he ever put this in writing?'

'I have a letter about the will,' she said.

'What about it?'

'Telling me about it. You see, he made a will leaving everything to Irene and then decided to make a second will leaving half to her and half to his son.'

'And what happened to that other will?' I asked.

She frowned thoughtfully and said: 'Wait a minute, Donald. I think *I* have it.'

'*You* do?'

She nodded.

'Take a look,' I said.

She went to a desk, opened a drawer, rummaged through some papers and said: 'Here it is.'

The paper read:

Having been advised that a will entirely written, dated, and signed in my handwriting is a good and valid will, I hereby make this My Last Will and Testament, leaving everything I have to Irene Addis. I intentionally make no provision for my son, Herbert Dowling, Jr., because I know his mother will take care of him. I revoke all other wills. I am a lonely man. Ever since I lost Irene I have been searching in vain, trying to find some woman who could take her place. Now I know there is no such woman. In all the world there is only one Irene. I tried to have the freedom which comes from living the life of a gay bachelor. Too late, I have come to realize that bachelors are inevitably lonely.

The will was signed *Herbert Jason Dowling*, and the date was ten days earlier.

I folded the will and put it in my pocket. 'You can testify this is in Dowling's handwriting?' I asked.

'Yes. Every bit of it. But, Donald, that will isn't any good because he executed this later one.'

I said: 'He executed the later will, and Bernice Clinton knew he was going to give that to Irene. She followed him to the motel. She shot him through the window, then went in and took the will from his body. She thought that by doing that she would reinstate the will she has; that she would then be free to force Carson to marry her; that she would have an independent fortune in her own name, a respectable position and social prestige.

'I knew we could knock out the will Bernice had by proving she murdered him, but I wasn't so sure about getting any property for Irene or proving the child was his. This last will does it.'

'Oh, I'm *so* glad!' she said.

'Are you?' I asked. 'You were making a play for him.'

'I told you that I threw in the sponge,' she said.

'When?'

'At the cafeteria that day.'

'That was when you first realized you were licked?'

'Yes. I knew I couldn't ever get to first base with him. I knew no other woman could ever fill the hunger that was eating into his soul. He might get physical satisfaction but spiritually he was mated to Irene Addis and always had been.

'I'm putting my cards on the table with you, Donald Lam, because I have an idea it's going to be better that way. You may think I'm a double-crossing schemer; perhaps I am. I think all women are when it comes to a question of marriage, security and respectability.'

I pulled out my notebook and started scribbling.

'What are you writing?' she asked.

'I'm giving you a receipt for this will,' I said.

I handed her the receipt and walked to the door.

Back in the office, Elsie Brand looked up when I came in and said: 'Well, where have you been? The most awful stories have been around, Donald, that you were in trouble.'

'I was.'

'Are you?'

'Not now.'

'Oh, Donald, I'm so glad!'

She came close to me, put her arms around me. Her lips came spontaneously to mine. 'Oh, Donald, I was so frightened, so terribly, terribly frightened. Bertha was fit to be tied.'

I said: 'Thanks for the concern, kid – and thanks for the kiss.'

215

'Thank *you*,' she said archly, 'and who, may I ask, is the young woman who gives the initials of *M-B-H*?'

'I wouldn't know.'

'There's a note,' she said, 'saying that the manager is all taken care of and that she is available any time. The note is signed *M-B-H*.'

'That,' I said, 'would be Miss Hines, who works at the telegraph office.'

'What's her first name?' she asked.

'Maybe,' I said.

'Maybe?'

'Maybe.'

'Well, this note sounds as though there wasn't any question about it.'

'What else is new?' I asked.

'That stripper, Daffidill Lawson.'

'What about her?'

'She called up. She has a sultry voice and she wished me to tell you she wanted to register *extreme* gratitude. She said you just couldn't imagine how grateful she was.'

'Grateful for what?'

'Your part in the publicity.'

'Anything come of it?'

'Anything come of it!' she said. 'She's been signed up on the Strip in Las Vegas for two weeks at ten grand a week.

'She says she's been made, thanks to you. . . . Donald, did you?'

'What?'

'Make her?'

I grinned and said: 'Back to your crime clippings, Sister. Bertha Cool will be in directly, and I've got to get an attorney on the line and get Irene Addis to file a petition for the probate of the last will and testament of Herbert Jason Dowling. The estate will probably reach a couple of million dollars by the time we've exposed Carson's intrigue in the company. I imagine our fee will be somewhere around a hundred grand.'

Elsie looked at me with wide, startled eyes. 'Donald!' she said, and came towards me in a whirlwind, her arms around me. 'Donald, you're wonderful!'

It was at that moment that Bertha Cool opened the door of the office.

She took in the tableau, said: 'Fry me for an oyster,' stepped back, closed the door gently behind her and went away.

Elsie, startled, said: 'Well, now you can fry *me* for an oyster!'

www.ingramcontent.com/pod-product-compliance
Ingram Content Group UK Ltd.
Pitfield, Milton Keynes, MK11 3LW, UK
UKHW022315280225
455674UK00004B/310